Bowen James had a ~~~~~~
When had that happened? How?
Oh, she knew how. But...

It hurt to swallow because her throat had dried. Heart pumping, she slapped a palm against her chest.

The man had a daughter. Which could only mean he must also have a wife. Or a girlfriend... Did the baby's mom know that Bo knew the real estate agent? That they'd had a thing years ago? A thing that had been so intense Kiara had actually hoped, at the time, it could become permanent? Her biological clock had been running down. She'd been so ready to commit, to start a family before it was too late. And she had loved Bo. Deeply.

But you were wrong. He wasn't the right man for you.

Shaking her head, Kiara wandered back and forth before the crib. Surprisingly, the girl had not stirred, even with their loud whispers. The scent of the baby reminded her of the one thing she could never have...

Dear Reader,

What do you believe makes a family? There are so many answers to that question. I loved exploring that question with my sexy martial arts fighter hero, Bowen James, and his adorable sidekick, Emily. Are their hearts open to allowing another person into their lives? Is the new girl on the block, Kiara Kirk, capable of stretching out of her self-imposed boundaries and embracing something she has always desired? I hope you enjoy this version of family!

Michele

The CEO and the Single Dad

Michele Renae

HARLEQUIN

Romance

HARLEQUIN®
Romance™

Recycling programs
for this product may
not exist in your area.

ISBN-13: 978-1-335-73707-6

The CEO and the Single Dad

Copyright © 2023 by Michele Hauf

For questions and comments about the quality of this book,
please contact us at CustomerService@Harlequin.com.

Harlequin Enterprises ULC
22 Adelaide St. West, 41st Floor
Toronto, Ontario M5H 4E3, Canada
www.Harlequin.com

Printed in U.S.A.

Michele Renae is the pseudonym for award-winning author Michele Hauf. She has published over ninety novels in historical, paranormal and contemporary romance and fantasy, as well as written action/adventure as Alex Archer. Instead of "writing what she knows," she prefers to write "what she would love to know and do" (and yes, that includes being a jewel thief and/or a brain surgeon).

You can email Michele at toastfaery@gmail.com.
Instagram: @MicheleHauf
Pinterest: @ToastFaery

Books by Michele Renae

Harlequin Romance

Cinderella's Second Chance in Paris

Visit the Author Profile page
at Harlequin.com.

Here's to wishes, dreams and aspirations.
May you touch them all.

CHAPTER ONE

KIARA KIRK CRINGED away from the hands slapping the driver's side window of her rental car. Half a dozen reporters and paparazzi milled outside the Swiss chalet where she had parked. She had an appointment to meet with the owner, MMA fighter and self-made millionaire Bowen James, to discuss selling the property.

Gripping the steering wheel, she summoned the courage to step outside and face the gauntlet of curious media.

"Not yet," she whispered. A moment to gather her wits was required.

Avoiding questions and blocking a photograph with a slash of her hand was not a problem. She'd experienced this crush of insanity six years earlier, when she had dated Bowen James. The media had an insatiable curiosity to learn who she was, why she was in his life and was she sleeping with him.

But the press hadn't been a factor in her walking away from Bowen. That had been a devastatingly emotional decision. The reason, which she'd locked away in a cage within her, fortified against emotion, must never be opened.

Kiara sold houses, chateaus, mansions and even the occasional medieval castle, all across Europe. A star on the realty scene, she had been recently dubbed by the press as the Queen of Luxury Real Estate. A much-deserved title, yet she avoided media like the plague. Wasn't her scene.

"Knocked for a loop" was the only way to describe getting a call from Bo after six years. They'd dated six months. *Six amazing months.* But had split because she felt there had been no other way to manage her life at that time. There had been no shouting, no angry accusations. Just a text. From her to Bowen. She'd changed her number. Moved out of London. And had not looked back.

Until today. For some reason that disturbed Kiara more than she cared to acknowledge, the desire she'd had for Bo had reemerged while talking to him on the phone. Once, he'd only had to glance at her and she'd lose it. Drop any work she had. Follow wherever he led. Want to tear away his clothes and tumble into bed with him. And they had. All the time, day or night, in a car, in a private jet, in a hotel room bed. They'd been at their best when having sex.

Despite their history, Kiara had said *yes* to representing Bo's house sale, and to helping him locate a new home in the French countryside. For two reasons. One, she rarely turned down representing a luxury property that was owned by a celebrity. Big money and visibility for her agency. She'd deal with the media; let them gab about the Queen of Luxury Real Estate all they wanted. Just make sure they spelled her name right and include a link to her website.

The second reason was personal. She wanted to see Bo again. To know that it had really, truly been a fast and furious time in her life that she never wanted to repeat.

But she needed to be careful—there was something about the Heartbreaker that still lived in her soul. He'd imprinted on her. All her best sex dreams featured Bo. And dreams about her future, living in the perfect home, seemed to focus on Bo lounging on a chair or smiling at her from a doorway. She never felt guilty for those dreams. But she also knew they were fantasy. Especially when the man had clearly stated family wasn't for him.

Fact remained, Bowen James had been the only man she'd ever loved.

An insistent knock on the window made her

wince. Her fingers twisted around the steering wheel.

"This is business," she said to the impeccably styled face in her rearview mirror. She had honed a steely resolve since she'd last seen Bo.

Giving a finger fluff to her bouncy mid-neck-length chestnut curls, she pursed her lips to check her rose velour lipstick. Eyebrows perfect. Blush contoured like a pro.

"Ready," she said.

Grabbing her briefcase and camera bag from the passenger seat, Kiara sized up the crew outside as they stood back and waited for her to make a move.

Opening the car door, she thrust out a long, tan leg. Her black leather Louboutin hit the asphalt. She stood in a graceful move that allowed her to tug down her short skirt at the same time she hooked the camera bag over her shoulder. The walk to the front door was thirty feet across what looked like heated concrete. Nice selling point. As well, the recessed lighting strip that lined the drive. She lifted her chin, and marched forward.

The reporters started in.

"Who are you?" one asked.

"Are you Bowen's girlfriend?" queried another.

"What can you tell us about his latest news?"

"Are you the one?"

"You look familiar."

"What's your name?"

"Come on, talk to us!"

They did not touch her. Surely, it was the chilly vibe she projected. Also, the risk of being charged with assault. The best way to play the press was to be coy. At least, until she got more comfortable with walking through the media circus.

About ten feet from the front door, the boisterous gaggle stopped, as if kept back by an invisible line.

Kiara pressed the security buzzer. The door opened. Kiara stepped in, but at the sight of the man before her, her shoulders hit the door. She blew at a strand of dark curls that had a tendency to tumble over one eye. And then she sucked in a breath.

Before her stood the sexiest man she had ever slept with. Tall, dark, lean and muscled like a prizefighter, Bowen James had not changed much in six years. The red velvet robe he wore, rimmed with fake tiger fur around the lapel, hung loosely to reveal his bare chest and...oh, those abs were so hard and tight. That one particular muscle that darted from a man's hips and down toward...mmm, right there. That had always been her favorite spot to linger.

Kiara tugged in her lower lip with her teeth. Holding the camera bag and her briefcase against her stomach felt like a barrier that she needed. Because if a man had ever looked jumpable, this one did. And she was not beyond making that jump, considering her last romp between the sheets had been months ago. However, that was not how the Queen of Luxury Real Estate began a relationship with a new client.

"Kiara!" Bo was famous for his good-natured personality, but she detected a tightness in his tone. "Look at you. I'm so happy you made the trip. The reporters didn't hassle you, did they?"

"I'm fine. Just forgot what your life is like. Do they drive all the way out here to bug you? It's twenty minutes from the closest town, and that wasn't even a town. More like a cozy village."

Bo shrugged, then shoved his hands in the robe pockets. His lanky posture and straight shoulders made him appear like a rock star who liked to grab the world by the throat, punch it, then step back with a teasing grin and challenge the return punch.

"I released some news yesterday," he offered. He had a heavy British accent that she'd always adored. "Newer news than the other news I put out last week. I figured they'd show up again. Took me days to get rid of them last week.

Sorry. I should have warned you. But come inside. Let me help you with your stuff."

As he took her bags, the skim of his fingers over hers pulsed a shock wave through her system. At one time, they'd been so perfect together. A touch from Bo would have invited her into his arms, no words necessary.

Bowen jumped down the two steps and strode into the living room, which was a vast, curved area faced with a two-story window that overlooked an expanse of lush summer forest. A long, black leather couch was situated opposite the window and must have sat twenty people. He tossed her stuff onto the couch.

"My God, Kiara, you look smashing. Your hair used to be so long."

She shrugged. "I like it this length." She'd cut off a foot after breaking up with him. More professional and easier to care for. A new start.

"I do, too," he said. "Shows off your pretty neck. But seriously? That dress?"

"What about my dress?" She played the innocent. But really, she'd spent an hour deciding what to wear today. The pumpkin-yellow bandage dress had won. It set off her tan and drew focus to her dark hair and full lips.

"It wraps your body tighter than I wrap my hands before a round." He took in her body. Admittedly, she was slender and hardly aspiring to cleavage, but she did appreciate her long legs and flat stomach. "It's a good thing I know you hate me, otherwise I'd have trouble keeping my hands off you."

And there it was. The perfect pair. Destroyed. "I don't—"

Before she could finish, Bo spun around the end of the couch and trekked toward the kitchen. He called back, "I need a drink! What can I get you? No alcohol in this house. But I might have lemonade. Or how about my protein punch?"

She was aware Bo had developed a line of protein powders and drinks, along with an entire clothing line, and martial arts equipment. He'd also jumped on the reality-TV-show circuit. He'd been busy since she'd last seen him. And he'd increased his wealth remarkably because of those deals, which hadn't required him to throw a single punch.

"Just water is fine," she called, thankful for a few moments to gather herself. The past was the past, right?

Hands on her hips, Kiara strolled to the window and surveyed the view. Below, a vast swath of green pines, spotted here and there with lighter maples, hugged the land. Bo's twenty-acre property was tucked amid a forest. He wanted to sell because the chalet was too remote. His goal was to be closer to a major city but still out in the country, and preferably closer to his mother, who lived in France. If Kiara owned a place like this, she might never return to civilization.

On the other hand, she was currently living in a fifth-floor, two-room apartment in Paris. If you could call checking in once every month or so, living in it. Most often, she stayed in hotels while traveling between clients and properties. And that suited her just fine.

Most of the time.

But hell, sometimes, she found herself craving some stability. A place to call home. It wasn't as though she'd didn't do a little shopping for herself when viewing properties with clients. She'd yet to find the one place that spoke to her heart.

Bowen returned to the room, leaped over the footrest at the end of the couch and set two bottles of water on the massive steel coffee table. He joined her before the window. Side by side. No touch this time. Marking his distance. To be expected, she decided.

"This view is incredible," Kiara said. "You sure you want to sell?"

"One hundred percent. Switzerland is nice, but this place doesn't fit my life anymore. Too many trees. And believe it or not, the internet is spotty."

She turned to find his eyes were as blue as she remembered. Like Sunday afternoons in the park and icy blue raspberry Popsicles. "What *is* your life like right now?"

He lifted his chin. An arrow gaze directed at her made her feel as if she was suddenly an opponent in the ring. "You want to get into it right away?"

They did have a lot to talk about. But really, now was not the time for a deep conversation. She'd just met him. Again. And she hadn't found her footing around him yet.

"Well, I did come here to assess the property," she said. "And, if I'm to find the perfect place for you, it helps to learn what's going on in your life and what you want for your future."

His gaze slid down her body. She could feel every molecule he breathed as he took her in. "You really care about my future, Duck?"

That single word melted her staunch determination and replaced it with a trickle of warm, melty desire. He'd called her "Duck" when they were dating. It was a weird nickname, but she'd never protested it. Bo was possessed of a sublime weirdness. As well, he had a habit of assigning certain people bird names. She'd never asked why. It was probably a British thing. The man had been born and raised in Brixton, London. Hadn't moved into the city proper until he was twenty-six and starting to make a name for himself on the fighting circuit.

"I'm not your duck anymore. And your future is a new home, so, yes, I do care. It's my job, Bo."

"All right, then. Bear said you were the Realtor of the moment, so I'm willing to play this real businesslike to get the job done."

Same. But seriously, she was very skilled at couching her emotions. It was a talent she'd developed since leaving Bo. So no more gawking at his tight muscles.

"You said you made an announcement yesterday? What was that?" she asked.

Bo bounced on his toes, the classic boxer's bounce, but his smile beamed as he spread his arms wide and announced, "I'm retiring!"

A mixture of shock, disappointment and a strange happiness swirled in Kiara's heart. The man had been on the fighting circuit for quite some time. He loved fighting. He'd once told her standing against an opponent in the ring was like breathing to him.

"Why?"

"My life has changed. I don't get anything out of beating my opponents in the ring anymore."

"Wow. You used to get a high from winning a fight."

"Most fighters do. But a lot of that comes

from a place of anger. Myself included. I'm not angry anymore, Kiara. And, well, I'm not a spring chicken, either."

"You're only…" She recalled he was a few years younger than her. "Thirty-six?"

"Thirty-seven. Pretty much the end of the game for MMA fighters. I mean, I have some good years left in me. But…no. Thanks to my investments, and playing the celebrity scene, I can afford to retire. And my contract is up so I'm ready to start something new."

"Like what, exactly?"

He spread his arms wide. "Everything! I want to move to a cozy farmhouse, plant a garden, build a barn, maybe get some goats."

"Goats—Bowen, are you kidding me? What's gotten into you?" The man used to spend what little money he'd had like water and seek crowds for their energy. And had the word *cozy* ever crossed his lips before? She peered at him with discernment. "I know you've always been concerned about brain damage…"

He chuckled. "I'm good. I was just in to see the doc a month ago. He said this hard skull of mine has kept me sane."

"Then I don't understand."

"Do you have to understand?" His sharp look slashed her pride like a blade. Not a bit of the goofy man in that gaze. "I'm not the same guy you dated six years ago, Kiara. I've changed. I'm less…"

"Angry?"

He pointed a finger at her. "I seem to recall, of the two of us, you had a very healthy angry streak. At least, you did in the end."

He recalled correctly. She'd never told him what it was that had made her rage against her very life and anyone who got in her path after she'd gotten some devastating news. Now? She'd moved on. Life was about the sell. And she was a master at it.

Nothing else mattered.

"I've chilled." She wandered over to the coffee table. After twisting open a bottle of water with Bo's Heartbreaker brand logo on it, she tilted back a swallow.

"I have, too." Bowen did the same. "I begin every day with yoga."

Kiara choked on a sip. She pressed the back of her hand to his forehead. "Now I'm certain I am not at the right house. Yoga? That's…"

So not the man she once knew. But he did sound just as interesting.

Bowen checked his watch. "I'm expecting a call from my manager any minute."

"No problem." She remembered those manager calls. Bo revered the man and thought of him much like a father. He'd never mentioned his real father to her when they were dating, except to dodge the subject of family whenever it arose. A clue she should have paid much closer attention to at the time. "I usually walk through the client's house to get a feel for it, then go back and do each room more thoroughly. I've set aside this afternoon and all of tomorrow for it. Can I take a look while you talk?"

"Of course. *Me casa es su casa*." His phone rang. "This is Marty. I've got to take it. Have at it, Duck!"

Kiara grabbed the water bottle, and as Bowen paced before the window, talking, she headed off to survey each room in the chalet. An irrepressible smile curled her mouth as she wandered into the kitchen. He was electric, as always. Handsome, as always. And smolderingly sexy.

But something had changed. Something inside Bowen James beamed out like a bright beacon. And she liked it.

CHAPTER TWO

Bo PEERED THROUGH the frosted glass set in the front door as he spoke to Marty O'Malley, his manager. The man was going on about how Bowen needed to take a year off. Reassess. Then he could come back and enjoy the sport again.

Outside, reporters loitered. They'd shown up hours earlier. He'd returned from a jog down the trail, spied the television vans and veered through the back door to avoid them. He had no problem talking to them. The pitfall of being a celebrity. Over the years he'd grown media-savvy. The challenge had been that leaked post two weeks earlier. A photographer had nabbed a pic of him and Emily. It had forced him to tell the world, via TikTok, about his family. Reporters had camped out two days until he'd finally realized they wouldn't leave without a sound bite from him.

"Bowen?"

"I'm here, Marty. Just figuring a game plan to face the press camped on my driveway. Dodge around and tease them, or go straight for the punch?"

"Don't elaborate. Just repeat what you've already said. But you could say you're giving retirement a try. That'll leave it open-ended for a return."

Marty would not give up. He wouldn't be a great manager if he did. The man had helped Bo rise from a no-name local gym fighter, to the UFC, to world championships. He'd been a friend, a brother, at times even a father to Bo. He'd helped Bo grow an investment portfolio that had made him a millionaire. He owed Marty a lot. Of course, the man received a handsome paycheck, so he didn't owe him monetarily.

"I'm determined to give this a go." Bo stepped back from the door window and paced toward the scenic view in his living room.

"I know. Life has tossed you a surprise. I give you a few months to play Mr. Mom then you'll be clamoring for a spot in the ring. All that sweat and blood. The energy of the fight. You need it, Bo. My door is always open, you know that."

"I do."

Bo glanced upward. A gorgeous woman wandered around his home, touching his things, assessing his living conditions, and…he wanted to send all the reporters home, tell Marty to go screw himself and then kiss Kiara like he'd never kissed her before. But really? Where would that get him? Did he *want* back a woman who had ghosted him after six months of bliss? She had literally disappeared from his life. And he wasn't prepared to step in that mess again.

His life had changed. He had responsibilities now. And he took that very seriously. Number one rule he must follow? Do not allow Kiara Kirk back into his heart.

He could follow that rule. But, man, that dress. It hugged her body and accentuated every curve, dimple and sweet spot. And Bo recalled she did have a lot of sweet spots. Places that when he kissed or brushed his lips against made her coo, squirm and even orgasm.

When he'd asked his friend Bear Bradford what Realtor he had used to find his chateau, Bear had given him Kiara's information. Bo had let that info sit on his phone for a week before finally summoning the courage to call her. Would she even answer? Would she bring up their devastating breakup? Would she tell him to go jump in a lake? Did he have the right to ask her for an explanation?

Or would he, as usual, feel like he deserved

such treatment because he was, after all, his father's son. Like it or not, Bo had learned to take punches, no matter the intent or the person they came from.

"Not anymore," he muttered. He wouldn't let any woman bring him down. He would make a good life for himself and his family.

"Bowen?"

"Huh? Oh, yeah, Marty, I gotta go. The Realtor is here. Don't want to keep her waiting on me."

"Let her do her thing. You go outside and talk to the press. Tell them you just want to take off a year—"

"I'm not going to change my mind, Marty. I'm sorry, but this feels right to me. I have to take a chance and see if this is what my heart needs."

"You're sounding all squishy right now, kid. I'll call you in a week and we'll talk again. It's never too late to change your mind."

"Sure thing, Marty. I'll send the press on their way with a couple of sound bites. Talk to you later." He clicked off.

Bo had been thinking about this for months. Fighting would only get in the way of his new life direction.

Grabbing the front door handle, he was about

to open it when a woman's voice called down from the second floor in a theatrical whisper.

"Bo!"

"What?"

"I've got a question for you!"

A damsel in distress? Much more interesting than facing the hungry paparazzi. He bounded up the stairs. Yet when he saw the doorway where Kiara was standing, Bo suddenly halted. Right. That room. He looked back down the stairs. Reporters or a curious Realtor?

"Bo?"

Well, she had to know. Everyone knew. Right?

Five minutes earlier...

Kiara answered a phone call as she strolled down the hallway. "Lyle. What's up?"

Her assistant/friend was currently stationed in New York while he cleaned out his recently deceased parents' apartment. Since Kiara had established her own agency they'd worked remotely. Kiara had met Lyle in a Parisian café. Lyle had complimented her on her tight ass, in a manner that only a gay man could make sound not creepy. Kiara had marveled over the man's spreadsheet on his open laptop. A genius with figures and schedules, Lyle had been looking for a job that didn't require him to punch in and work out of a cubicle.

"Are you at Bowen James's chalet?" Lyle asked.

"Of course. You know I have an appointment here today. You still in New York?"

"Flying back to Paris this evening. There's something I think you need to know about our Mr. James, Kiara."

Pausing in the open doorway to a room, Kiara peered inside. Odd. This was not another normal bedroom. She wandered inside, her attention distracted.

"Kiara?" Lyle said insistently.

"What is it, Lyle? I'm in the process of going through the house…"

The curtains were drawn and the room was dark, but not so dim that she couldn't see the few items of furniture. She stepped forward and bent to exam what turned out to be a massive stuffed bear sitting on the floor.

"This is…" she muttered. What was a giant toy doing in the home of a professional MMA fighter? And…the furniture?

"It's about Bowen," Lyle said. "Did you follow his socials?"

"Not yet. I haven't had time." She stepped back. Her shoe nudged something covered in plastic. It looked like a pack of…diapers? And behind her, in a crib... Kiara snuck closer. A baby slumbered inside the crib!

Jaw dropping open, Kiara pressed a palm to her mouth. What was a—a baby...?

"Well, this is kind of important for you to know considering what you told me that one time—"

"I have to go, Lyle," she whispered. "There's something weird going on here. Talk soon!"

Clicking off, Kiara leaned over the crib to study the infant. Yes, it was a real baby. Dressed in a pink onesie. Sleeping peacefully, despite her conversation with Lyle. Was Bo...babysitting?

According to everything she knew about Bowen James, that made zero sense.

She rushed from the room and at the top of the stairs started to call out, then adjusted her voice to a loud whisper.

Wandering down the hallway toward the woman who clung to the doorframe, Bo couldn't decide if she looked happy, angry, or freaked out.

"Bo, I need to know what, exactly, well..." She gestured inside the room.

He shoved his hands in the robe pockets. He'd not dressed since his jog. Some days he wore his shorts and robe all day. Why not? He lived in the almost middle of nowhere. And the reporters that occasionally camped on his front steps never breeched the front door.

Kiara's lush scent reached out and grabbed him. She always smelled tropical and sun-warmed. And she looked it in that stunner dress. Like sunshine molded into the shape of a woman.

Drawn into her aura, but keeping his hands in his pockets, Bo leaned a shoulder against the doorjamb and peered inside the room. That night he'd been called to the hospital had changed his life. But a kind nurse, suspecting his utter shock, had sat down with him and helped him surf an online upscale baby retailer. The next day everything had arrived to furnish this room—a crib, a big comfy chair, a couple of hampers and a dresser filled with crib sheets and onesies. Baby toys sat here and there. He loved that giant stuffed bear with the googly eyes. More than a few times he'd fallen asleep sitting on the floor against the thing. He'd awaken wrapped in the bear's arms.

"What does it look like to you?" he asked.

"Seriously? Bo, there's a baby in the crib."

"And I hope she's still sleeping."

"She is. I checked, but… Bo! Focus!"

"I am focused. On you. You smell so good, Kiara. You know what that scent on your skin does to me."

"I do." She huffed. Smoothed her palms over

the tight fabric. Something was different about her. She was less…open. More stiff. Composed. Not a hair out of place. And she purposely stood with her body facing away from him.

If anyone had the right to harbor anger, of the two of them, it was him. Nice-smelling or not. He had to be careful around her. And never forget the rule.

"You're getting off the subject," she said. "Why is there a baby in this room?"

"Emily has to sleep somewhere." A bang on the front door distracted him from Kiara's gaping expression. "The natives are getting restless. I should go down and give them what they want before they get too loud and wake her."

"Bo, wait," she whispered loudly.

"What?"

"Emily?"

"That's her name." He shrugged. "Don't you follow my socials?"

She lifted her phone and frantically tapped the screen. "Lyle just said the same thing."

"Who's Lyle?"

"My assistant. What is going on? What am I missing?"

"You don't follow me?" Affront felt more appropriate than anger right now. "Shouldn't following your clients be necessary?"

"I do, but I haven't had time yet to follow you— Oh."

He waited while she scrolled. He posted on the socials about once a week. Mostly fun stuff like training moves, tricks and tips. Yesterday he'd posted about his retirement. A week ago? He'd decided it was time, after six months, to post about Emily.

Kiara spread her arms in wonder. Obviously, she had no clue about his announcement. The woman deserved an explanation. So why did it feel so hard to explain right now? It felt almost as awkward as he had felt that night he'd gotten the call from the Bern police, requesting he come to the hospital immediately. Only to arrive and learn he was a new father.

"Emily is your…?" Kiara asked.

A wild hoot erupted from outside. What were those reporters up to? Stepping back and toward the stairs, Bo said, "She's my daughter."

"Your…" She scrolled again. "There are no photos of a… A baby?"

"Never," he said firmly. "I'd never put photos of my child out there for the world. That's a blatant breach of privacy. I plan to protect her with my life. I have to go calm the crowd outside, Duck. I'm sorry. Give me a few!"

He waved and fled the tense discussion that he knew would follow. Right now, he had to deal with one disturbance before he could focus on the other.

* * *

Kiara stood in the threshold to the nursery. Emily? His *daughter*?

And yet, apparently Bo had told the world about it a week earlier on social media.

Throat drying, she glanced around the dim room. A box labeled with a photo of a baby mobile sat near the window, unopened. A stack of plastic-wrapped diapers tilted against another wall. A baby monitor sat on the table next to the crib, beside a bunny rattle and a folded blanket.

And a sleeping baby.

Bowen James had a baby? When had that happened? How? Oh, she knew *how*. But… But!

It hurt to swallow because her throat had dried. Heart pumping, she slapped a palm against her chest.

The man had a daughter. Which could only mean he must also have a wife. Or a girlfriend. Someone had to have given birth to the precious baby lying not three feet from her. Had the mother gone out while Bo handled the details with the Realtor? Did the baby's mom know that Bo knew her? That they'd had a thing years ago? A thing that had been so intense Kiara had actually hoped, at the time, it could become permanent? Her biological clock had been running down. She'd been so ready to commit, to start a

family, before it was too late. And she had loved
Bo. Deeply.

*But you were wrong. He wasn't the right man
for you.*

Shaking her head, Kiara wandered back and
forth in front of the crib. Surprisingly, the baby
had not stirred, even with their loud whispers.
The scent of talcum reminded her of the one
thing she could never have.

Of all the people she'd never expected to reveal a baby, Bowen James topped that list. One
of the last things he'd said to her before he'd left
for his big fight in New York six years ago had
been "I'll never be a father." It had been in response to her telling him she was ready to commit, to have a family with him.

Kiara exhaled heavily. She would not hyper-
ventilate. This news—this baby—had nothing
to do with her life now. She was beyond that
disappointment.

"So he's got a baby," she whispered. A glance
to the crib stretched a wistful tightness across
her face. "Good for him. Right?"

She reached toward the crib. That part of
her that she'd decided to control six years ago
strained for release…

Kiara snapped back her hand.

*Avoid babies. They will only dredge up the
devastating hurt.*

She backed toward the doorway. The urge to get out of this room was at the forefront of her mind. And to get out of the house was also a strong thought. But she remembered the reporters outside. She didn't want to struggle through that tussle with her thoughts in such chaos. Bo had said they'd leave after he spoke to them.

Out in the hallway, Kiara leaned her shoulders against the wall and tilted back her head. "He's a daddy."

Good for him.

And in the next moment she couldn't fight back the longing that always struck her hard whenever she was around babies. Bo had a baby.

And she did not.

CHAPTER THREE

KIARA COLLECTED HER briefcase and camera bag from the leather couch. She hadn't walked through the entire house because after seeing the nursery her brain had switched from business mode to what-the-hell? mode. She needed a breather.

The front door closed. She looked up to see Bo leaning against it, exhaling purposefully. The man actually did yoga now? She could get behind some enlightenment. But a baby? It was too bizarre to wrap her brain around.

He gave her the okay sign with his fingers. Then gestured with one finger for a pause. Bags held at the ready for her escape, Kiara stopped. She heard an engine start. The reporters must be leaving.

Bo relaxed, bounced on his toes a few times, then threw a few playful punches. His way of coming down from anything that caused him anxiety. His body was fluid, and assorted muscles flexed and…a man had no right being so sexy.

When he stopped, he said to her, "Are you going somewhere? I thought you had to assess the house? You can't be finished already."

"I'm not done. I just…" Need some space! "I'll return tomorrow to take measurements and notes on each room and the land. I have to go." She checked the nonexistent watch on her bare wrist. "Have some phone calls to make. Have to schedule a photographer for the sell sheet. Line up the staging crew." All Lyle's responsibility, but the lie felt necessary right now.

"You can make the calls here. I'll give you privacy. You can use the office. The reporters are heading out, if that's what's troubling you. I gave them a statement. Though, they were really curious about you."

Kiara hung her head and let her shoulders drop. The last thing she'd expected when driving up to the chalet had been to walk into a scandal. "What did they want to know about me? You did tell them we are not dating."

"I didn't say a thing. My manager always says the less said, the better. They did wonder if you were Emily's mother, though."

Oh, God, she had to get out of here! Kiara veered around the end of the couch and up the two steps to the main floor of the kitchen and foyer. Bo remained by the door.

"I want to leave before…you know…" She winced.

Bo made show of bending to look at something on the kitchen counter. A baby monitor, which she'd not noticed previously. The light was green. No sound came from it. "It's okay. She's a sound sleeper. You don't need to rush off."

Walking back into Bo's life had been a mistake. She never could have anticipated how his life had changed or how it would affect her on an emotional level. Right now her heart thundered and tears threatened. She must not cry!

"But what about your wife or girlfriend? Aren't they coming home soon?"

"Kiara." Bo bridged their distance. She looked over his shoulder. The door, and her escape from this crazy moment, was so close. "There's no girlfriend. And certainly not a wife."

"Oh. But then how did you get a—" Kiara winced. She didn't want to be crass or cruel. But none of this made sense. "I'm just curious about how Bowen James came to have a baby."

Bo closed his eyes. Kiara sensed an immediate change from sincere longing over his absent child to a tightness that reminded her of his fighting mode.

"I'm sorry, did I say something wrong?"

"Emily's mom is dead."

The camera bag dropped and landed beside Kiara's shoe. Oh, dear. That was horrible. Tragic. She'd stepped into some deep territory. And was not prepared for this heavy conversation.

"I don't know what to say. I'm sorry, Bo."

"Me, too. I'll tell you about it sometime," he said, "but right now I need to change the tone of the room. I'm reading some very tense vibes on you, Kiara. That's not good for your health."

She hadn't forgotten the man was a stickler for all things healthy, be it food, exercise, or mental clarity. Counter that with his fits of anger and goofy streaks? He had certainly been a unique boyfriend. And lover.

Mercy, she couldn't allow herself to go there. Not to their past. It had been really good. Like a forever-commitment good. Until she had fled.

"Are you up for pizza for dinner?" he asked. "We might have a chance to eat alone before Emily wakes. She's usually up in about an hour."

"Pizza? Bo, how can you think of food when—"

"It happened six months ago, Kiara. Emily. And her mom dying. And apparently you don't have a clue since you don't follow me on the socials."

"I do now," she protested.

What a stupid argument to have! He'd lost Emily's mother. The man must be grief-stricken. But instead, he wanted to make pizza? Perhaps it was his means of dealing with the loss. She'd never lost anyone close. She had no clue how grief worked.

Best to follow his lead.

"Pizza sounds great," she said. She was hungry, having downed only coffee on the drive here from the airport. "But really, I shouldn't stay. I planned to stay in the village tonight. I'm sure I can find a B-and-B. I can return in the morning to work up the details on the house. It'll take most of the day."

"I insist you stay here. It's quieter, and more comfortable than the rooms above the only pub in the village. You did see the guest room?"

She had. It featured a king-size bed, gorgeous southern light and all-white furnishings. Sort of like sleeping inside a cloud, she'd thought. No way had Bo furnished that room. He had obviously paid a mint to bring in a designer.

"I couldn't."

"You can. And there's still a few reporters lingering outside. Do you really want to go out there?"

"I thought you gave them what they wanted?"

"I did. But I suspect they want info on you."

"Ugh."

"Let's do pizza. I make it myself. I promise it'll change your religion."

"Seriously?" This all felt so out-of-sync with the news he'd just laid on her. And yet, he was handling it fine. Six months? So he'd had some time to deal with it. But she had just found out.

No. Kiara! This is not your problem to own, worry about, or solve. Let it go. You focus on the sale.

"Yep. It's a veggie-and-cauliflower crust—hey, don't give me that face. It is so good."

"I remember you are a superclean eater."

"Can't win a fight unless I treat my body right." He flexed a bicep.

The topic change was needed. But with a glance upward, toward the nursery, Kiara really did want to know about Emily's mother. Bo was a rogue, a playboy. It was the reason he'd been labeled with the Heartbreaker nickname early in his career when he'd dated a few female fighters. He'd rarely dated anyone more than a few days or weeks. Their six months had been his longest relationship. At the time, she'd garnered a weird bit of pride in that.

Obviously, some woman had won over his heart long enough to have a baby by the man who had sworn never to start a family.

"Let me get started on pizza. Do you want to go back to work or are you done for the day?"

Kiara glanced to the front door. If the reporters were still out there it made little sense to try for an escape. And she did need to finish the initial run-through. Fleeing because she'd learned about Bo's baby was not good business practice. She would remain. Everything was good. At least, she would pull on the emotional armor and make it look good. It was a talent she'd honed since she was young and her mother had worked all hours of the day, often forgetting she even had a daughter.

"There are a few rooms I've yet to wander into on this main floor," Kiara said. "And I want to look over the backyard and surrounding land and make notes before the sun sets. Will the reporters see me out there?"

"No, the security wall blocks the backyard. But you might want to avoid the front yard for a while. There's an awesome path out front that cuts through the forest on my property. I jog it every morning."

"What sort of wild beasts live out here?"

He shrugged. "I don't know. Wolves. Bears. Lots of raccoons."

"I think I'll pass on the path through the woods. Will I be safe in the backyard?"

"Yep. The wild beasties only come out at

night." He waggled his eyebrows and winked at her.

Kiara almost smiled at his joke. Almost. Because she wasn't sure if it had been a joke. "Unless you need me to help you with dinner?"

"Do what you need to do, Miss Queen of Luxury Real Estate. I'll do my best to wine and dine you."

"Sounds…" Promising. "Much better than a room above a noisy bar."

"You know it. So you'll stay the night?" He didn't need the eyebrow waggle this time; it was that charming glint in his raspberry-Popsicle eyes that gave him away.

Oh, Kiara, this could prove dangerous. Foolish. Unwise. Heart-wrenching.

Exciting.

"Yes." She left the room and headed outside before she could change her mind. Staying in the house with Bo would challenge her desires. But staying in the house with a baby? That would challenge her heart and soul.

The pizza was out of this world. The wine Bo had brought up from the cellar was sweet. The lighting was low. The music was an instrumental cello band that played everything from orchestral arrangements to heavy metal covers. And the man laughing right now held Kiara rapt. Bo was so fluid in his movements. He embodied every single bone, which could be attributed to his training. Martial arts was a sport that relied on quick reactions and the ability to fluctuate between varied defensive and offensive positions, and the use of the whole body.

Yet he was laughing at his daughter. He'd brought down Emily from her nap before dishing up the pizza. The baby hadn't wanted a bottle, so he'd laid her on a blanket beneath a baby gym and she was currently kicking the bright plastic danglers.

"Doesn't that giggle make you laugh?" Bo glanced to Kiara.

She nodded, despite her need to not lose herself in observing the baby. But who wouldn't get lost in the utter joy of a six-month-old exploring their toes and the newfound ability to kick at things? Emily was adorable. And that made Kiara's heart ache. So she focused on Bo instead.

Those deep all-seeing eyes that had held contact with her whenever possible as their bodies had merged and their sighs had mingled. She could look into them all day… Kiara sighed. He was looking at her. Taking her in. Reading her—

She suddenly sat upright. The half-eaten pizza slice in her hand forgotten. She tossed it to the plate. Smoothed her hand along the linen napkin on her lap.

"Were you just in another world, Duck?"

He possessed a mischievous little-boy grin that bordered on naughty-grown-man territory. He knew it and utilized it to his advantage.

Kiara swore softly and then shrugged. "Maybe. Yes. I'm sorry. Emily is so cute. But you've got… It's your eyes."

He narrowed them "I do have eyes."

"They are gorgeous, Bo. I've told you that before. It's difficult for a woman not to lose herself in them."

"Yeah? But you were more than lost just now. You were entertaining thoughts. Sexy thoughts?" He waggled his dark eyebrows. Leaning forward on the couch, he set his plate on the table. "I mean, it's not like I haven't thought about you. A lot. Wondered what you're up to. If you still hate me."

"I never hated you, Bo." Plate forgotten on her lap, Kiara settled back on the large easy chair and stared up at the ceiling. "It was just…some strange anger that I had at the time. It got misdirected at you."

"That's the part that confused me." He reached over and tapped the bright red plastic butterfly, giving Emily a swaying target. "You were always pretty easygoing, Duck. What were you so angry about?"

Life had kicked her hard and it had hurt. Who wouldn't get angry over that?

"I don't want to talk about it."

He rubbed the heel of his palm over his brow and huffed. "You didn't want to talk about it then. All I got was a text message. Hell, Kiara, you ghosted me. That was not classy. Whatever made you run? You must still be angry about it."

"I seem to recall you not wanting to talk about things, either, Bo."

He sighed heavily. "You wanted to talk about some heavy stuff just as I was leaving. The limo was waiting. I did promise we'd talk once I got back from the fight."

She did remember that. Unfortunately, life had intervened. She'd had to leave. It had felt like the only option at the time. "I said I don't want to talk about it."

"Whatever you want," Bo said. "But just so you know, Kiara? I never cheated on you. I would never do that to any woman." He crossed a finger over his chest. "Cross my heart."

"Sure."

"You don't believe me? What does a guy have to do? I know it was that crazy magazine lay-out that set you off because that was the first thing I saw when I got home to my London flat.

Kiara, you know that was posed. I told you all about it after I got home from the job. I didn't even know those women."

The layout in question had been a four-page article featuring a centerfold spread of Bo wearing his boxer shorts and world-championship gold belt, lying across a group of half-naked women. Some facing upward, others downward. Kiara distinctly recalled one of his hands had landed across a random breast, the other across a woman's thigh. It had been tastefully done, but also, it had been borderline explicit. It had played with his reputation of being a ladies man. At the time Bo had argued it had been fun but not his idea.

The magazine had arrived while he had been away for the New York fight, and she had opened it. The image had infuriated Kiara. She'd seen it the morning before she'd gone into the emergency room. It had upset her. But she'd not for a moment suspected he'd been unfaithful to her. It was just one more thing to make her question Bo. To make her realize he couldn't give her the life she had wanted then. And she knew that he hadn't had sex with any of them. He was a flirtatious, charming Casanova, but he was also respectful of women.

Protect your heart, Kiara. You've changed.

You've built up emotional armor. Just like your mother. Use it.

"Let's talk about something else." Kiara tilted back a swallow of wine, then held out her empty goblet.

Bo handed the wine bottle to her. "Avoiding your issues? Not very grown-up, Duck."

She gaped, prepared to defend herself, but… he wasn't wrong.

"Why are you retiring?" she quickly asked. Change of topic was the best way to avoid the truths she couldn't handle right now. "Is it because of the baby?"

"Of course, but also, I'm not getting any younger."

"You're only thirty-seven. You're not Methuselah."

"I know, but my knee crunches from ACL tears, my arm has been hyperextended more times than I can remember, I've lost half a dozen teeth and my nose can't handle being broken one more time. I've only got a few more good years in me before my body completely falls to pieces."

"Then why not take those years? You can pay for a nanny. Single dads all across the world make it work."

"Yeah, but a single dad with brain damage would not be cool. There's not a lot of fighters who make it out of the profession without some kind of brain injury. I've had plenty of concussions. My doc keeps warning me the next could be the one to change my life. So that's a good reason. Don't you think?"

"Of course. I didn't know about the concussions." She recalled he'd only been in two fights during the time they'd dated. The second had been when she'd ran off. She'd specifically waited until the day following his winning fight to text him that they were over. It would have been doubly cruel to deliver bad news before his fight. "You shouldn't take the risk. Especially not when you've got a daughter."

"Yes, and Emily is my other reason for retirement." He leaned over the blanket and nuzzled his nose against Emily's belly. "She's the most adorable little chicken in the world." The baby let out a squeal of giggles. Bo sat back on his knees. "I've never been so in love."

He was genuinely passionate about his daughter. It was a beautiful thing to see. If also surprising.

"Never in a million years would I have imagined myself as a parent, but here I am." He splayed out his arms. "Doing the diaper-and-bottle routine. Four a.m. feedings? I am a pro. Who coordinates pink bows with pink socks? This guy. I can also sing all of 'Baby Monkey.'

Over and over. It's the only song Emily wants to hear when we're in the car. And I'm loving every minute of it."

"You don't have a nanny? You're doing this all by yourself?"

He nodded.

"That's amazing. I mean, I recall you telling me you had no desire to become…"

To become a father. He'd casually mentioned it a few times when they'd been together, but he'd brushed it off as something he'd never given much thought to. So when Kiara had decided to open her heart to him and confess she thought they should think about committing, becoming a real family and having children, she'd expected they could discuss it. How devastating it had felt to hear him confirm he was dead set against becoming a father. It had hit her heart like a physical punch.

But if he was giving her rein with not talking about her reason for ghosting him, then she could do the same for him.

"You've didn't have siblings, from what I recall you telling me when we dated," she said. "So taking care of a baby just…came naturally?"

"Not at all. I kept putting the diapers on backward. Didn't realize my mistake until a few days later when my mum arrived to help. I mean, seriously, they should label those things front and back. Anyway, Mum gave me lots of tips. But also..." He tugged out his phone. "YouTube and TikTok. I joined a bunch of single-dad groups. I've learned a lot. And I have to say I'm not too shabby at this dad stuff. So far, Emily hasn't complained."

To have a baby to take care of, to learn to meet her every need, and to watch her grow and love her. Kiara's heart fluttered. That's what dreams were made of! But at the same time her core tightened. It didn't feel fair. This man had implicitly not wanted children.

"So can you tell me about Emily's mother?"

Bo sighed. After a few bites of pizza, he put up his feet on the coffee table and spread his arms across the back of the sofa. "It was a result of traumatic injuries from a car crash. Happened about fifteen minutes after Emily was born. I dated Jennifer for about a week. I couldn't even call it dating, more like— You know how I am."

"I do." He had hooked up with Jennifer for a week of sex and then they had gone their separate ways. No commitments. No strings. The Heartbreaker at his finest.

"Jen and I had a good time, then split," Bo continued. "No animosity, no arguments. I went on with my life, always training, talking to Marty about getting some work on reality

TV shows to fill the time between fights. You know I like to stay busy. Anyway, I had a couple fights last winter, and then out of the blue I get a phone call from the local police in Bern. It was an emergency about Jennifer. So I hopped in the car and drove there. When I arrived the doctors told me that Jen and her fiancé had been in a car accident. The nurse told me he died instantly, but Jen had held on long enough to safely deliver her baby. I arrived just in time... Jen saw me. Smiled. Clasped my hand... Then she passed away."

"Oh, my God." Tears wobbled in Kiara's eyes. What a horrible experience for Bo. And the baby's mother.

He nodded. "She didn't have family beyond her fiancé. I was Emily's only family."

Pressing her fingers over her mouth, Kiara kept the tears from falling. But just barely.

"It was a shock to me. But the hospital does DNA testing and they were able to confirm Emily was mine. Not that I doubted it. It was standard procedure in order for me to take her home."

Kiara nodded silently.

"I wasn't sure about taking her home. One of the nurses sat with me after she put Emily in my arms. She talked so softly. I don't remember half the stuff she said to me, but I recall the way she made me feel. Safe. Reassured. I think she kept me from going into shock. And in those moments I found some breathing room. And you know what? I fell in love with Emily. Didn't give a moment to considering leaving without her." He sighed and stretched his arms out over his head. "That was six months ago. The first few days home with the baby I fumbled through every movement. Thought for sure I'd drop her. But Emily was remarkable with me. So patient."

"Seriously?"

"Yeah, it was like she knew I didn't know what the heck to do with her. And she just gave me these big patient eyes. Like 'I'm starving, Daddy, but I know you'll get the milk just right before you feed me.'" He rubbed his jaw and shook his head. "Lately, she likes to sleep in. Can you believe that?"

Kiara hadn't cared for an infant since her teenaged babysitting years. But she'd always thought the first few months were sleepless nights and night of the living parents.

"Every day I fall more and more in love with my Chicken." He used his toe to waggle the infant's diaper-padded behind, which caused her to giggle again. "I never imagined I, Bowen James, would be doing the dad thing, let alone doing it all on my own. But here I am."

"Here you are."

The man had taken a one-eighty, not by his own choosing, but what a remarkable move. To walk out of the hospital with a newborn baby and a whole new life? He seemed to have embraced the situation. Hell, he appeared to be thriving in the new role. And that the infant had been placed into her biological father's arms was incredible. Yet, why hadn't Jennifer chosen to tell Bo about the pregnancy and start a life with him?

"You didn't consider—" Kiara coached her tone to a soft kindness "—putting her up for adoption?"

"Never crossed my mind. Emily is my daughter. Family means everything to me."

"It does?" Kiara checked her tone, which had just taken a sharp rise. Really, that did not sound like Bowen James. At all. "I guess I didn't know that about you." Because he'd made it clear to her he'd felt the opposite. "Well, I know you still have your mother. Do you see her often?"

"Often as I can. We get together for birthdays and holidays. Mum's got a boyfriend now," Bo said. "Some French charmer who lured her out of London. He's good for her. And the country life makes her happy. You just don't know how good it makes me feel to see her smile and laugh. That was a long time coming."

Kiara recalled Bo had alluded to his mom

struggling in an abusive marriage. He'd never said more than that, always keeping his past locked tight. Kiara couldn't imagine living in an abusive relationship. She was thankful her childhood had been normal and downright uneventful. So her mother had been busy creating her career and hugs had been few. And okay, there had been more than many times Katherine Kirk would forget to pick up her daughter from dance classes, Brownies, or even movie night. Kiara had survived, and in the process, had learned to take care of herself. And following Katherine Kirk's example had put her where she stood today. At the top of the real-estate market.

"What does your mother think about you popping an instant grandchild on her?"

"Mum was over the moon. She is excited about being a grandmum."

"I bet. Single parenting is a tough job, Bo. And with all your other commitments?"

"Hence, retirement. I think it'll be good for me and Emily. But now we need to dump this over-the-top bachelor pad. I want something smaller but with more usable land. I still want trees, but not an entire forest."

"I have two properties picked out for you in the Caen area. I'll have Lyle see to arranging some viewings quickly. You said Bear Bradford is the one who gave you my name?"

"Yep. We're good friends."

"One of the properties is not far from where he is living now. Lots of trees and the chateau isn't so large."

"I don't need big. I do need child-friendly. A place where Emily can run barefoot outside and play. But I do need a room for my gym."

"I'll look through my files for the info and have it to you by tomorrow. I seem to recall there was a vineyard on the property."

"I don't need vines. That sounds like a lot of upkeep."

"Yes. But let me look into it. If that doesn't work, I've a few other places currently in my arsenal."

"Sounds like you know what you're doing. And if it's close to Caen even better because that's where mom is. You were just getting started with real estate when we dated. Weren't you on some kind of time-share vacation when we met?"

"Yes, I was working with a luxury agency in the States. My boss had convinced me to take two weeks in London as reward for a big sale. I, uh, extended that vacation."

After the two weeks, when she'd faced returning home to sell properties in the US, Kiara had known, without doubt, that was not her future. She'd always loved traveling. Every summer, as a child, her dad would take her to a new country for a vacation. Katherine usually had business to tend to; she'd never been one for vacations. And Kiara's real-estate goals included eventually moving out of the States and growing her dreams internationally. As well, she had met Bo during that first week and wanted to spend as much time with him as possible. So she'd called her boss and told him she wanted to stay. He couldn't keep her on staff, but had recommended her to a London agency. She'd interviewed with them while dating Bo, and had gotten a referral call to join their Paris branch about a week after she'd left Bo. The call had come at a time when she'd needed redirection and a focus. She'd kissed her dad goodbye and hopped on a plane, and hadn't looked back since.

"Now look at you." Bo's voice lured her from her memories. "Fancy shoes and big-bucks clients. You're even getting inches on the celebrity sites."

Kiara lifted her chin and shrugged. "I don't enjoy the media attention. I'm rather private." But lately, Lyle had been prodding her to get comfortable with that scene. And the press had been sniffing around the agency due to their multimillion-dollar sales. "But I know those inches are good for sales. Every celebrity I help to find a home gets me more clients. It's how I play the game. I have worked hard for this. And I deserve it."

"As I deserve this retirement."

He did need a break if he intended to raise a child on his own. And to live closer to his mother, who could help him with that? Kiara would do her best to find him the perfect home to bring up Emily.

"You said you had the floor plans for this place? If you could find those that would help me tremendously."

"I think they're in the attic."

"Let me clean up the dinner dishes while you look." She glanced out the window. Twilight hazed the sky to a metallic sheen. "I do my best work burning the midnight oil."

"I'll be right back. Keep an eye on Emily, will you?" He winked and strolled out of the room.

Kiara looked at the baby on the floor. Her muscles tensed. Half of her wanted to run away, put herself as far from the wide-eyed fascination and silly giggles as possible. The other half of her wanted to clutch Emily to her breast and inhale her sweet smell. Fulfill a dream she'd had shattered years ago.

Bo couldn't possibly understand how difficult it was to be in the same room as a baby. If she was going to get through the next days and help him sell this house and find a new one, she would have to face those truths she'd hidden for so long. It was only fair to Bo. But she had no idea how to do so without completely losing control. And if she'd gained one thing over the years, it was control over a life that would fall apart without it.

"Not going to pick you up," she whispered.

Kiara closed her eyes. What had she gotten herself into?

CHAPTER FOUR

Bo rounded the curve on the paved trail that veered him back toward the chalet. He reduced his running speed to a jog. He always ran full speed for the first leg, then slowed to bring down his heart rate during the return trip.

It was five in the morning. He could see his breaths before him in the chilled air. Soon enough, the Swiss mountains would warm up to a sultry summer day. He loved these quiet morning jogs, but hadn't been able to get out as often since Emily had come into his life. He did have a jogging stroller but she was not an early riser like him. Go figure!

He checked the baby monitor on his wrist. Green was good to go, no stirring yet. He never went far with Emily alone in the house. Anything could happen. Running at top speed, he could return to the chalet in a few minutes.

He was incorporating Emily into his life with much more ease than he'd imagined possible.

Well. He'd never imagined having a baby in his life. And being a single father? Not in a million years. But just because the mechanics of taking care of an infant seemed to move smoothly didn't mean the emotional gears glided as freely. What the hell was he doing? Thinking he could do the daddy thing? He had absolutely no idea how to handle stuff like tears and boo-boos. And what about when she started to walk, and then talk, and then dating?

Bo punched the air, shadowboxing as he slowed his pace more. His father had been no role model, that was for sure. Killian James was an example of how not to be a father. And every moment Bo felt a muscle tense, because he wasn't sure how to react to Emily's cries, he wondered if he would become his dad.

Rule number two: never become Killian James.

"You." He delivered an air punch. "Are." A swift uppercut. "Not." And a bruising hook to the jaw. "Him."

How could the man have ever held a baby in his arms, and then one day decide it was okay to harm that child? It was something Bo couldn't understand, having held Emily against his chest and felt her heart beat against his. No one would ever harm his daughter.

Including himself.

Despite the sudden lifestyle upheaval, he hadn't spent a moment cursing the surprise of Emily. She was the new girl in his life. And he wouldn't change that for all the martial arts titles in the world.

But now, the new surprise. Kiara. Not even a surprise. He had invited her back into his life believing she would be the best person to help him and Emily find a new home. She had been obviously taken aback to discover Emily's room.

Was she happy for him? Confused? Angry?

Kiara was a hard read. Yet, she'd never been like that. When they had dated it was as though they could read each other's thoughts. Anticipate what the other needed: a kiss, a hug, a walk holding hands, hot sex in a restaurant loo.

It had been six years. And while he'd been madly in love with her—so much so that he'd bought an engagement ring while in New York for the big fight—and could feel all those old emotions rising again, Bo had to keep cautioning himself to walk a wide circle around her. She'd broken his heart. Torn it out and stomped on it. Mercilessly. And now, she didn't seem to be overly concerned about that emotional destruction.

He could still recall her text. He'd read it so many times, it had burned into his memory.

This isn't working. You can never commit. I know you don't want a family. Sorry. I've already moved out.

He'd never told her about growing up with an abusive father. A man just didn't talk about things like that. It was the reason why he didn't want a family. *Hadn't* wanted a family.

How things had changed.

And here she was, back in his life. The real heartbreaker. He'd expected an apology. At the very least, an explanation for her departure. And a chance to talk. About everything.

Maybe she needed a few days to get comfortable with him again. He wanted to get the chalet on the market while she was here. With hope, his mom could take Emily while they looked for new houses.

But damn, it was difficult not to recall their past. He wanted Kiara. He didn't want her. Yes, he could sleep with her, have a fling, then push her out and close the door behind her. That was his MO.

Bo shook his head. Not anymore. Because Emily was his girl now. And Bo intended to give her the best life. A life without fear of her own father. And if Kiara wanted to give his daughter a run for his emotional currency, she could try, but she would never win.

What had he done? He'd invited the one woman who had altered his life irreversibly back into his home. Kiara had once shown him what stability could look like, a different view of the world. And he'd bought in to that shiny view. But he wasn't sure if his newly softened heart would be strong enough to endure another emotional upset. Because he'd lost his trust in Kiara Kirk.

Kiara woke, showered in the guest bathroom, then slipped into something more comfortable than the body-hugging yellow number she'd worn yesterday. to be honest with herself? Yesterday she'd wanted to draw Bo's attention. Today? She needed to resume business mode. She'd packed a sundress with pink florals set against a red background. It still hugged her body, but it went to her knees and the pattern was busy enough to distract from things she didn't necessarily want Bo eyeballing.

"You don't need his approval or his eyes on your nonexistent A-cups," she muttered to her reflection in the bathroom mirror. "You just need the commission for selling this house. And the media interest that comes along with it. And do not let that cute little baby soften your heart."

She had to stay on top of her game. *If you slow down, you lose.* Her mom had taught her that. Katherine Kirk must be proud of what her daughter had accomplished. Right? She would never come out and actually give Kiara a compliment, but she did let Kiara know she was following her career and that she was on the right track. A track Kiara had never imagined she'd be on. Because at one time she had been all about starting a family, in defiance of her mother's expectations.

How life changed.

After checking her hair in the mirror and finishing her lipstick—she always wore rose velour; it was her color—she stepped back and eyed the bedroom door that opened to the hallway.

Bo was out there. She'd heard him return from a morning workout. The sun hadn't risen when she'd first heard him up and about, but it had now. She hadn't intended to spend the night.

On the other hand, what a night. The moment her cheek had hit the pillow and she wrapped herself in the luxurious sheets, she'd drifted to the Land of Nod. The man did know how to treat his guests right. The Egyptian cotton was a far cry from the rough sheets he'd once had in his London apartment.

In just six short years, Bowen James had climbed from MMA fighting champion who couldn't afford a luxury car or home, to millionaire bad-boy heartbreaker of the reality-TV set. Amazing.

She hadn't thought Bo was the type who would sell his soul by appearing on those television shows, but apparently that had changed about him as well. He'd once been focused on the fight, unconcerned that the UFC was not a place where he could make millions. He'd fought because he loved it. And now he was retiring. Which wasn't the end of the world. He'd obviously made enough money to support himself in comfort, and even luxury. And she certainly didn't want him injuring himself to the extent it changed him physically or mentally. Emily needed a strong, sound father.

How would being a single dad change him?

She didn't want to know. It wasn't important. She had to focus on the job, help him find a new home, then drive out of his life. Again.

Kiara let out a breath and whispered, "Don't do that to him again. Be...nice."

Yes, she could do that. She didn't have to make a big thing of his being a father. It needn't affect her. They could be friends. Right?

"Friends with benefits?" she muttered, then shook her head. "Stop thinking about him that way. It's too dangerous to your heart."

Exactly. Because a fling would never be just that.

While Kiara's biological clock had broken a

spring years ago, the few remaining gears that turned and progressed her through life were pushing her toward finding the missing piece to the stability puzzle. She had the million-dollar career. Now, she wanted a place to call home. And soft sheets to snuggle between, next to someone she loved. The word *marriage* may even fit into that puzzle.

Bowen could never be that missing piece.

And yet, now he'd somehow put himself back on that list of possibilities for her.

She shook her head. "Not for me. For himself. It's his family. Not mine." So work it was.

Gathering her laptop and camera, she decided to begin in this room. Measurements, details about materials, the windows, et cetera, all had to be noted. This chalet would sell, no problem. But she liked to make sure she knew the property like the back of her hand so no oddball question from a potential buyer could throw her off. And her file for this home must be detailed so that the other two agents with Kirk Prestige Homes could read it and know the property as well.

Today, she would learn this home.

By midafternoon, Bo couldn't stand it anymore. He'd given Kiara space to do her thing. But that cute flowered dress, and her long legs, and the way her hair fell over her face when she leaned forward to type something on her laptop?

He squeezed the lemon he'd cut over the arugula salad, but winced as the juice splayed over his wrist. Whoops! Too much. He'd been distracted by the stretch of Kiara's arm as she reached to glide her tape measure along the scenic window in the living room. And the arch of her back. That sleek soft area behind her ear that was now exposed as her hair tumbled to the side...

Emily's loud burp tugged him out of his admiration. "Seriously?" he asked his daughter, who sat in the high chair beside him. Then in a whisper he added, "Not the best way to impress the pretty lady." And louder, he called across the room, "All the measurements should be on the blueprint." He licked the sour juice from his fingers and wrist, then bowed to kiss Emily's head.

"I know. But I like to double-check. And I'm learning the house as I do this manually. That smells great."

"It's steamed tofu seasoned with a spice mix from my product line. I created it myself."

"Quite the homemaker you've become."

She strode along the window, her attention on the laptop. Did she realize those high heels made her legs look twice as long and...he wanted them wrapped around his back?

Emily's burble redirected his focus. Right. Only one girl in his life right now.

"You'd make the perfect catch," Kiara called, unaware of his distraction. "Cooks, takes care of children, can protect you with a mean punch to the liver. But do you clean?"

Bo laughed. "Have you seen the mess in Emily's room?"

"I have. But seriously, if that minor clutter is what you call a mess I'm worried about you."

"How so?"

She paused and glanced his way. Those lush long lashes drew attention to her dark brown eyes. "That you've become domesticated."

Bo opened the air fryer, which was placed on the opposite counter, far from Emily, and checked the tofu. Perfection. He pulled out the perforated basket. "What's wrong with that?"

"Nothing." She wandered toward the couch and began measuring that. "Is all the furniture remaining?"

"Yes. No. I'll take the baby stuff with me. Emily would really miss that big stuffed bear." Him, even more. "Everything else can stay. That couch is monstrous, and ugly." And he distinctly recalled his hot-and-heavy night with Jen, right there. He could never tell Emily she had been conceived on a leather couch. The indignity!

"I'm not completely domesticated. There's more to me than diapers and baby spit-up."

"This is real leather, right?"

"Of course, it is. So who cares if I'm a family man now, anyway?"

She shrugged. "Your next ex-girlfriend?"

Low blow. She knew him too well. And yet… "If she likes me she won't become an ex."

Kiara straightened and regarded him. That lipstick was so…come-and-taste-me pink. She'd never worn lipstick when they were dating… "So you're looking for a long-term relationship now? I suppose you've got to find a mother for Emily."

"That's not it." Was it?

That was exactly what his mother had also suggested. Being raised by a mom and dad would only be fair to Emily. Bo wasn't so sure yet. He was still finding his feet with the father thing. He strived to be kind and attentive. But he had to admit some days were crazy challenges of lost binkies, unwashed blankies and that day he'd run out of diapers and had to wrap a towel around Emily for the trip to the store— Oi!

"I do know you weren't big on family," Kiara stated. "You said, 'No kids, not ever,' if I recall correctly."

The last time they spoke, she'd asked him if

he'd ever change his mind about children. Because she was ready to commit. He'd answered as always, with an abrupt *no*. He should have explained himself. But the limo had been waiting to take him to the airport. Would his life have gone differently if he had told her then and there his reason behind not wanting to be a father?

"I've changed, Kiara. A lot."

"You most certainly have." She walked up to the kitchen counter and slid onto a barstool, her attention still glued to the laptop as she clicked away on it. She didn't place herself next to Emily. Seemed sort of skittish around her, actually. And had yet to ask to hold her. Bo wouldn't press. She was probably in work mode. And yet, for a woman who had dreamed of having children, he was surprised she wasn't all over Emily.

He didn't care. He wasn't going to date a woman because she liked him for having a baby and imagined herself becoming Emily's mom and living happily ever after. Nor would he date a woman who thought she could take advantage of his bank account and live the high life without concern for his daughter's needs.

But he did want to date. To find...the one. Because the more he'd done the love-'em-and-leave-'em, the more that had made him realize such an MO wasn't working anymore. He liked being in a relationship. For the adult conversation. For the connection. And, bloody hell, for the sex! He literally had not had sex since Emily had come into his life.

"Do *you* think I've changed for the better?" He tossed the seasoned tofu in with the salad greens, then added pepper and crushed pistachios.

Kiara clicked away, her focus intense on the screen. That lipstick drew his eye like an arrow to the target.

"Kiara?"

"Huh?"

"Right." Not paying him any mind. Totally over him. Probably turned off by the baby spit-up on his shoulder. He could take a hint.

Besides, she'd already given him the biggest hint ever. He'd never forget that text. He'd been brought to his knees, literally.

Protect your heart, he reminded himself. For Emily's sake.

"Time for a lunch break. You going to join us?"

"Sounds great." *Click, click, click.* "Give me a few minutes."

Twenty minutes later, after he'd finished his portion and had fed Emily pears, spinach and a full bottle, Kiara finally pushed aside her laptop and pulled her untouched plate toward her.

"You never used to be like this," Bo said as he patted Emily's back. Her head rested against his shoulder and he'd assumed the baby-rock motion that had initially surprised him. Whenever he held a sleepy Emily, the gentle, calming bounce motion automatically kicked in.

"Like what?" She forked in a bite, nodded her approval and forked up some more.

"So focused on work that you forget to eat. To hold a conversation with someone who obviously wants to talk with you. To even give Emily a glance when she's obviously trying her best to splatter the world with pears."

"Oh. Well, Bo, I am here on business."

"I get that. But now it's time to break for lunch. Eat. Take care of yourself."

"You think I don't take care of myself?"

"Seriously? I'm not sure. You used to be on the same page as me with the healthy eating, jogging, and…" Lots of physical activity, like sex.

"I feel great, Bo. And I do take care of myself."

"Really? How?"

She shrugged and continued to eat. "We can't all be athletes. My schedule is too busy for workouts. I eat…the right foods."

"You don't cook for yourself?" he asked.

"No time. I eat at nice restaurants. Do take-out."

"Kiara, that stuff is garbage."

"Yes, well, even if I can afford to hire a chef, I'm never home to make it worth it. I travel a lot. I don't have time for that…stuff."

"Stuff being self-care?"

She set down her fork and sipped the lemonade, then asked, "What do you care?"

"I'm always concerned about a person taking care of themselves. I stand behind my product line of protein drinks and super seasonings. And the workout course was derived from my personal regimen. Being good to your body is good for your soul, your brain."

"Like taking punches for a living is good for you?"

Yet another low blow. The woman still harbored some serious anger issues. Against him? Had she seen the darkness in him that he worried could rise and he would emulate his father? It was a stupid thought, but he chased it often. Is that why she left him?

After downing her drink in two long sips, Kiara then pushed away her plate and stood. "I have to get back to it. I appreciate the lunch. It was really good. But if I don't get back to work I won't finish by sunset."

"You can stay another day."

"Bo, this job should only take a day. I'm headed toward the gym now. To measure things, not break a sweat."

He slid a hand into hers as she passed him and stopped her with an abrupt tug. Kiara reared back, giving him an offended look. "What?"

"I really do feel as if I've changed," he said to her, "for the better."

Her mouth compressed, then softened. Her eyes took in Emily, now asleep against his chest. "You have," she said softly. "It's remarkable. *You* are remarkable."

When she made to walk away, he slid up his hand and gripped her arm gently. "Then give me a chance. I'm not asking you to fall in love or anything. I just want you to treat me like a person who is not a client. A friend."

She tugged from him and stepped back. "I'm sorry. I just… It's weird being here. Don't you think it's weird? The two of us together again? And…your baby."

"It's superweird. But Emily's not weird. She's just a little chicken. Does she bother you?"

"No, I didn't mean it that way. She's adorable. It's us."

"I know. After all this time, here we are again. It is awkward. But it also feels pretty good. And

I can't lie to you and say that every time I look at you I don't want to—"

"Don't say it, Bo. Please? Because..."

"Because you feel it, too?"

She winced, but then nodded. Bo's heart thundered. She was on the same page as him. At least concerning their physical desires.

"I didn't want to take this job," she said. "But I also did."

"I know that feeling."

"I thought..."

"*You* thought? Kiara, it was the hardest thing I've ever done, calling you about selling the chalet. I thought for sure you'd reject me, not speak to me. Again." He moved closer to her. Her soft perfume smelled like fruit and all the sweet things in the world. "I never stopped thinking about you, Kiara. I..."

Did he still love her? He could never go there without an explanation as to why she left him. And if it was because of what he said about not wanting to be a father...well, couldn't she see now that had been flipped on its head?

But did he really have the emotional capacity to allow her into his heart again? And right now? He had a daughter who needed his attention. Trying to start things with Kiara again would be like juggling two fireballs and not burn off all his hair. And some satisfying sex was not worth that heartache.

"I've thought about you a lot, too," she finally said. "I owe you some answers. But I'm not ready for that conversation yet. This mixing my work and…well, us."

Bo put up a hand placatingly. "I want to hear those answers. But I'm not going to push. Or expect anything from you. You do you, Kiara. And I don't want to screw up your work or get you in trouble with the boss—"

"I am the boss," she said firmly. "And I have to set an example for my employees."

"Who are—" he made show of looking around "—not here?"

She exhaled. "You know what I mean."

"I get it. But you can't work all day. When you punch out tonight, then you have to give me Kiara Kirk and not the Real Estate Queen. Deal?"

"Depends."

"On what?"

"On what you're making for dinner."

He caught her real smile this time and that made Bo laugh. "Whatever you desire, Duck. I'll make it. I'm free and…" He almost said *frisky*. He'd save that mood for later. When he trusted her. "Just let me know if you need help with anything. I'm going to put Emily down for a nap."

"You can go through the garage and back courtyard with me. Explain what things remain and what you'll be taking with you."

Bo lifted Emily from the high chair. "I'll be out in ten."

The six-car garage was usual for luxury properties. Kiara had once sold a property that had included a twenty-two-car garage! Now she didn't blink an eye at the heated floors and car lift, even the indoor shop, which seemed to contain every auto part a man may need should he have issues with his vehicles.

Bo owned six cars. That was not so much insane as unnecessary. When they'd dated he'd only owned the twenty-year-old VW. Yellow, of all colors!

While walking the sidewalk from the garage to the backyard, where a basketball court reigned, Kiara clicked out of her phone's notes app.

"Why the excess?" she asked. "I know you've become a millionaire, but why does a man need six cars?"

Bo laughed. "I have the SUV for driving to events and to the shore. The Jeep is for off-road-ing. The Mustang is for taking apart and putting back together. The Mini is what I drive to the village to pick up milk. The Audi has the car seat in it; it's Emily's ride. And the Ferrari is vintage."

"But you can only drive one at a time. I can never understand why rich people think they need so many cars. It's not even a status thing."

"It's not, but it's also fun to drive a different car every day. And after I started to pile up the cash from my TV appearances and investments I had to find ways to spend it. I'm a guy, Kiara. Let me have my cars. I'm not asking you about all your shoes, because I do recall you had a thing for shoes."

"Touché." She still didn't have the space to own all the shoes she'd like to have. Probably a good thing. Not even probably— most definitely.

She stopped before the court. The green, artificial-wood surface and white boundary lines were pristine. The backboard behind the hoop looked fresh out of the box. "I've never known you to shoot hoops."

"I don't. It came with the property. But I don't use it for dribbling. Check this out."

He hit a button on a panel at the wall to his side. Then he checked the monitor band on his wrist. Green light. Emily was sleeping. Grabbing her hand, he directed her to step back onto the rubber-padded area, where a couple of heavy bags hung as something remarkable happened. The floor of the court receded, downward, and was filled with water. It took about three minutes for the full court to be replaced by a swimming pool.

"Blows your mind, yeah?" Bo asked.

Kiara shrugged. "I've seen moving floor pools before. It is impressive, though. Definitely adds dollar signs to your asking price. What do you want to get for this property, anyway?"

"I paid ten million for it."

"That was a steal."

"Right? So I wouldn't mind fifteen this time."

"From what I've assessed so far, I can do you better and start it at eighteen."

"Nice." He held up his hand for her to slap and... Bo pouted. "Oh, come on, Duck. Give me some skin."

Fine! Kiara met him in a high five. And then he took her hand and skipped her around the pool toward the house, where the lanai was furnished with a single lane for bowling, two fireplaces, a massive bar and a retracting sunroof.

"Time to take a break," he said.

"You and all your breaks! I've only got the land to walk and then I'm finished."

"Sure, and I'll walk with you. But you need some refreshment. How about a celery shake?"

"Are you kidding me? There's no way you could have made that sound the least bit appetizing?"

"I can splash a little guava in there. Guava is the color of your lipstick, you know that? It's pink and so…"

Kiara mentally filled in the word he was probably thinking. Kissable? Yes, she remembered kissing him. Oh, the man could kiss. And to have another, just one, felt too luxurious, such a treat. But it was never just one kiss with this man. She knew that well enough. And— Wait a second, she *was* the boss.

In an instant, Kiara's heart slammed the door on her logic and turned her on her Louboutins. She marched up to Bo. Pushed her fingers through his hair, and pulled him to her for a kiss.

A hard one. A kiss that reminded her what she had run away from. A kiss that coaxed her with promises of a return to that amazing time in her life, when things had been carefree and she had thought she'd found the perfect man.

And she had.

That was the problem. Bo was too good for her.

Breaking their connection, Kiara stepped

back. She'd taken him by surprise. Not an easy thing to do with a man who trained for every unexpected move.

When a grin peeled across Bo's mouth, she knew she'd hit on that goofy boy who lived inside the man and would never grow up and always wanted to make life fun. Now, when he moved closer, she let him wrap her in his embrace and accepted the kiss for what it was. A long time coming. A "hello, how are you?" after too long. A dangerous foray into territory she'd long thought she'd closed the door on. Feeling. Caring for someone. Caring what she did for herself. Sharing herself with another person.

Well. She didn't have to share everything. And a kiss was all this would be. Just a kiss.

But as she hugged up against Bo's hard muscles, and her nipples peaked beneath the cotton dress, Kiara knew she'd made a mistake. One she could not correct.

And she wasn't sure she wanted to.

Their separation was gentler this time. Kiara stepped back, studying Bo's expression. His eyes were still closed, his mouth working into a slow smile. God, she'd loved him at one time. And it wasn't difficult to see how that had happened.

And yet…no. Just for the sake of her sanity, no!

She turned and walked into the house, even as Bo called after her.

"So…what? You're like the boss lady now? You call all the shots? Heh. I like it." He whistled a wolf call.

And Kiara smiled, despite herself.

CHAPTER FIVE

"I've arranged a viewing for you on Saturday at two separate but close properties west of Caen," Kiara said to Bo as he strolled into the kitchen, bouncing Emily.

The man wore only running shorts and that red robe trimmed with fake fur. A weird combo, but it was totally Bo. She had heard him punching the heavy bag after she'd walked away from their kiss. Working off some sexual frustration? That part hadn't changed about him.

"Doesn't Emily prefer you to shower after a workout?" she asked as he strapped the baby into the high chair, then began assembling fruits and powders for what she assumed would be a funky protein recovery shake.

"I just did," he said, looking offended.

"You're all wet. Don't you dry off?"

"It's nice to air-dry." He gave his head a shake and water droplets from his hair flicked across her face and top. "Besides, when my girl calls,

I go running. She has me wrapped around her little finger, don't you, Chicken?" He bowed to kiss the baby on the top of the head.

Kiara wiped the drops from her laptop screen. "So is Saturday good for you?"

"It's great. We can hop on a plane, be there in an hour. I called my mum. She'll be happy to look after Emily while we look at houses. They're not too big, are they?"

"No. And they both have a lot of acreage, so your neighbors are distant."

"I like that. But not too far away?"

"No more than a kilometer, I'd say. Lyle is still compiling the specs for me to verify."

She'd just gotten off the phone with Lyle. He'd insisted she take advantage of the media circus should they again camp out in front of the chalet. What a way to showcase Kirk Prestige Homes—showing her working for the millionaire Heartbreaker!

That thought had been at the back of her mind before even accepting the job. But since learning about Bo's daughter, Kiara wasn't so sure playing with the press's interest in their relationship would be wise. Or helpful to her agency. Bad press was not always better than no press at all.

"A security fence is on one of the properties," she said. "One of them has a pool, but it doesn't disappear into a basketball court. I think they'll both appeal to your need for an open space, but also offer privacy without the muffling perimeter of a thick forest."

"You've already dialed into my needs. I like that."

"It's my job, Bo. Don't read too much into it."

"I won't, boss lady." He smirked and pushed the blend button.

Boss lady was what he'd called her after she'd kissed him. And walked away on her own terms. And that was how it was going to play between them. On her terms.

But, oh, that kiss. It was as if the two of them were made for one another. The kiss had felt so natural, and they fit. Their bodies had hugged against one another, like... *Oh, yeah, I remember this place...here is where I belong.*

But admitting she would like—no, she needed—another kiss would never happen out loud. It couldn't. There was too much at stake now. She wasn't about to hurt Bo again, especially with another female involved. That female who went by the name of Emily, and who was currently vocalizing at the top of her lungs in accompaniment to the blender. Bo pushed a button to stop it. The baby stopped. Start. More shouting. The two of them laughed at their antics.

Kiara felt like an outsider who wasn't in on the joke. Did she want in on it? Maybe.

No. She wasn't here to play house. She was here to sell it.

Kiara texted the homeowners—both sets were out of town vacationing—to inform them they would be viewing the properties on Saturday. She inquired about local places to stay and one owner offered to let her stay at the property. They were in the States doing the Route 66 drive and wouldn't be back in France for a month. She thanked them and said she would consider it. But it wasn't her style to crash at a property.

"This recipe is Emily's favorite. Want some?" Bo held the blender up to display the olive-green contents.

"Hard pass."

"So what's the plan while we wait out Saturday?" He scooped out a spoonful into a bowl for his daughter, then drank straight from the blender. He offered her a green-mustached smile before swiping it away with a dish towel. "Want to hike with us this evening?"

"I didn't bring hiking clothes. Or shoes. And I've to meet with the photographer, who should arrive here in an hour to go through the house. I've got paperwork and financial forms to work up as well. Should keep me busy the rest of the day."

"Don't you have a secretary to do that kind of stuff?"

"Lyle does do that kind of stuff, but I fill out the preliminaries for him to follow. I like to have a hand in every aspect of my business. It's smart. I am the CEO, after all."

He set down the pitcher and leaned on the counter. "I'm impressed by what you've done with your life, Kiara."

"I've been focused since…" Since she had walked away from him. More like run away. Her dream had always been family. And it had been stolen from her. And at the time, it had felt necessary to run, to just put herself away from the one hope she'd had for starting that family.

Now? She wasn't so sure that method of breakup had been wisest. For either of their hearts. Because, apparently, Bo was very capable of change. Should she have given him a chance?

Kiara sighed. "It's taken a lot of hard work to get to where I am. Lots of schmoozing and getting to know the right people, getting them to trust me. I keep an elite client list, and they know that I only deal in quality. Luxury. The unobtainable. And now I'm at the top."

"The top is a fine place to be. Been there. Done that. Fine with not returning. But tell me you're not doing it all alone," Bo said. "Do you… have a boyfriend?"

Kiara scoffed.

"You don't have time, I suppose. Not that you need a man. Looks like life is treating you well. It's just, you used to be much…calmer. More happy. Is being at the top worth it?"

"Of course, it is." The man had no idea what made her happy.

Was she happy? Happiness was so…ineffable.

He shrugged. "Riches mean nothing if you can't also enjoy the simpler things in life."

"Simple? I'm not inclined to buy six cars and bachelor pads with moving floor pools to satisfy my unmet emotional needs."

"Don't forget the private jet."

"You own a private jet? Why don't we fly that to the viewings?"

"I sold it. Do you know how expensive it is to maintain a jet? You have to rent a hanger, a pilot, gas, licenses, all kinds of accoutrements. It was ridiculous. I'm over the material stuff now. Give me celery juice and a giggly baby and I am a happy man."

Kiara cautioned herself from sighing. Because then he'd know she wasn't happy at the top. She was fulfilled. But was fulfillment the same as happiness? Certainly, it must be. She'd never thought about it much. Slowing down and allowing her brain to consider her personal needs was not easy to do. Well, it didn't fit the new protocol she'd assumed in order to thrive at the top. And who needed simple when fast and focused served her well enough?

"If the photographer doesn't arrive for a while," Bo said, "then you and I and Chicken are going for a walk."

"But you just got in from a workout."

"Don't you want to walk with us, Kiara? Take in the fresh air? Experience the beauty of the forest? I would expect a professional like you to take in all aspects of the property."

He had a point. But… "What about the beasties?"

"I'll protect you."

"You think a punch to a bear's mug is going to send it fleeing?"

"Probably not. But you have to be more worried about the racoons than the bears. Don't worry. I would never bring Emily into a dangerous situation. No bears. Promise."

Kiara glanced to Emily. The baby smashed her hand into the bowl of green smoothie. That's exactly how Kiara felt about hiking. It would be much messier than it appeared.

"Meet us out back," Bo said. "I'm sure you brought along some shoes that don't have mile-high spikes on the heels. It'll be an easy stroll." He winked and gathered up Emily, and after washing her hands in the sink, left to go change her diaper.

Kiara did have some sandals she schlepped along on her travels, because after a day in heels relief was a necessity. But they would not be appropriate for a hike through the woods.

She shuddered. This activity did not sound like a picnic. But for some reason she couldn't summon a single excuse not to spend time with Bo and Emily out in nature. When had she last enjoyed fresh air? Something...simple?

"You're not going to enjoy it," she said. "Because then you'll start wanting to take vacations. And that is not part of the protocol."

She closed her laptop and figured the sundress she wore was going to be the best bet for a walk. She'd bring along her camera. Grab some outdoor shots so the photographer wouldn't have to venture beyond the house. It would be a sneaky way to get some work done while appeasing Bo's need to see her go on an *easy stroll*.

Easy? She could smell a lie when she heard it. But, hell, when a sexy man invited her to a stroll through a forest, then she could soften her armor just a little and dive in, right?

Bo would have never asked Kiara on the walk had the trails been unmarked or even dirt pathways. This trail had been paved decades earlier by the former owner of the chalet. It wove through the forest and across a fresh spring, then back toward the house. It was three kilometers in length, but by the time they reached the turn-back he was glad it wasn't any longer. He was fit and could do this trail ten times over without breaking a sweat.

But sexy gladiator sandals and a sundress needed a rest.

Kiara showed surprise and relief to see the bench carved from a massive oak tree. She plopped down and Bo sat beside her, parking the jogging stroller so Emily's view was optimal. The overlook was perfectly placed. A person could take in the vast forest that angled on a gentle slope downward and, with a turn of the head, see the snow-capped glacial ski slopes to the north.

"It's beautiful out here. I'm taking some photos to use for the sell packets. Save the photographer a trip out here." She lifted her camera, which was hanging from the strap around her neck, and stood. Clicking away, she turned as she took in the view. "Emily seems so content."

"She loves walking in nature," Bo said.

He was happy that Kiara showed interest in his daughter. Though, still no desire to pick her up. If Kiara had such a fervent desire to have kids, as he'd known she did when they were dating, then he didn't understand why she only observed Emily from a distance. Almost as if she would drop her should she pick her up.

Been there. Did *not* do that. But he'd felt for sure, that first week or so, he might drop Emily. Babies seemed so fragile! Yet he knew, from bouncing her and playing airplane, she loved physical activity.

"We saw a reindeer a couple weeks ago," he added. "Emily thought it was awesome."

"As long as there are no bears." Kiara set down her camera and sat next to him again. "So it's all diapers and workouts lately? No extra-curricular social activities?"

"Like what?"

"I don't know. Going places where other adults are. Catching a movie. Dating."

Bo laughed because it was ridiculous to imagine arranging for any of those things now. "Would if I could, but the woman in my life is not cool with it." He toggled the dangling star hanging from the stroller canopy and Emily swiped at it.

"Emily doesn't know how lucky she is to have such a devoted dad. But have you ever considered that maybe some time away from her is good? Time to just…be the man you are? I mean, don't you want to date? To…"

Bo gently put his palms over Emily's ears. "To have sex? Is that what you're wondering?"

"I wasn't thinking...well. I suppose it's difficult to meet women living out here. And if you're not fighting anymore then you don't get out in public and..."

"Yes, I miss sex," he announced. "I haven't had sex since I took Emily into my home. But believe me, no time does not equate to no desire." He removed his hands.

He knew his daughter couldn't understand what he was talking about. But still, it wasn't right to talk about such things around children.

"You've got the time now. Oh." Kiara sat upright, clinging to the bench edge with tense fingers. "Well, I mean— I didn't mean to imply—"

"That we should have...you know?"

She was flustered? So not the spur-of-the-moment Kiara he'd once dated. Suggest sex to her and she would already have her dress off and be in the process of pulling his pants down. "I get what you mean, Duck. I was on you about self-care earlier. I guess that means I should pay closer attention to my own needs. But it's different with my Chicken. I'm not going to do the hookups anymore. Any woman I bring to bed..."

She waited for him to finish, but he realized to finish that sentence would imply he was testing dates for potential mom material. Which wasn't sexy at all. And not even true. He could do a one-night stand and not expect anything beyond the physical. He *needed* a one-nighter. But Kiara didn't need to know that. Because she hadn't earned that from him yet. He was still waiting on her *answers*.

"I have to say something to you," he said. There would never be a good time for this confession. But at least out here, he felt sure she wouldn't run from him. And if she did, he'd catch up to her quickly. "About us. What we were. You breaking it off with me the way you did."

Her fingers curled inward on her lap. Much as she held the smile on her face, he knew it was not a real one. When had she become so controlled?

"So that's why you took me all the way out here."

"Oh, come on, Kiara, I'm not that cruel. I just need you to know… When we were dating? You were everything to me." So much so, he'd bought an engagement ring. "I loved you so much."

"I did, too," she said softly.

"Then what did I do wrong? It was that argument, wasn't it? It wasn't even an argument. You just started talking about family and stuff and, well…"

"I had to know for sure. You'd given me enough hints that you never wanted a family."

"I know, but— And I had to leave fast because…" The limo had been waiting. Bo exhaled. He would never look good, no matter from what angle a person viewed their last argument. "You didn't even wait until I got home from New York to talk to me. Do you know how devastating it was to walk into my flat and find you gone? You'd taken the part of you that fit perfectly in my heart and excised it like a surgeon."

She opened her mouth but didn't say anything. Tough to hear the truth? Well, truth was all they had now. He no longer wanted to live by misunderstandings, or unspoken secrets. Life required honesty. And trust.

He leaned back and raked his fingers through his hair. "You hurt me, Kiara."

Her heavy sigh seeped through his pores. She was holding something within and he really needed to know what it was. He had grown up in an abusive household. He'd dodged his father's fists. Often. He'd watched that same man gamble away the family's savings. Go out with other women. Come home drunk. Repeat. And always, those words his father would shout at Bo lived in his memory—*You're just like me, Bowen. Bad to the bone.*

If Kiara didn't tell him why she'd left, it would only confirm what he'd always known. That he was truly bad to the bone and the blood of his father ran through his veins. That whatever had made Kiara leave had been his fault. Should he tell her about his childhood? What he'd survived? It wouldn't change things. Or make her understand how it had literally directed his life.

And yet, it was his truth.

"Kiara?"

"Fine, I'll tell you. What I can."

"What you can? So you're not going to tell me everything?"

"Bo, just listen. This is difficult for me. This…"

"Being honest with another person? Talking? I feel as though you've put up some armor since I last saw you, Kiara. And not just because of right here, right now. You've worn it for a while."

Another heavy sigh told him he'd been spot-on with that summation.

"It's necessary for the job. I have to compete with some high-level agents, and they are all men. I can't allow my emotions to reveal a weakness or it will cost me a client."

"I can understand that. For your job. But this is not work right now, Duck. This is me and you." And Emily. She had dozed off. Her head slightly tilted forward. She would be fine while they talked. And that Kiara wanted to talk was something. "We had something years ago. A something that's never left my bones. You're still in me. Just tell me why you fled. Please?"

"I had to leave, Bo. I couldn't stay. My life had turned upside down. I needed to be…away from everything and everyone."

Bo sat up straight. That sounded much heavier than he'd expected. Now he really needed to hear this. "Tell me."

The sadness in her eyes was so evident. The sparkle was gone. Her mouth could not smile, even if forced. And maybe that was a tear? Bloody hell, he hated to see her hurting. How to make it stop?

"I had just found out that I could not carry a child to term. That I'd never be able to have children," she said quickly.

Bo swore inwardly. The one woman whose only dream had been to have a family couldn't have one?

Bo was momentarily speechless.

"It shattered me," she said quietly. "I had to leave. I didn't want to talk to you about it because I knew how you felt about having children. You'd said over and over you never wanted to have a family."

He rubbed a hand over his hair. Yes, that idiot he had once been. Because having a family would mean he'd be a bad father, like his father had been. And he didn't want to repeat the sins of the father.

"I had a certain plan for my life, and that included having a family. I needed to...control that," Kiara said.

There was that word again: control. Bo felt sure Kiara didn't realize how much control she had and how it stifled her. It had changed her. To a successful businesswoman, which was nothing to sneeze at. But in trade, the soft, sweet woman had gotten trampled. Or, maybe...buried.

"I couldn't stay, Bo. I hope you can understand. I had to be alone. Or at least, get out of London. Clear my head. I went home to stay with my parents a few weeks. Well, my dad. Mom was away on a business trip. I had to sort out and get beyond the one thing that I had only ever wanted my entire life."

She sucked in a breath and exhaled, her back hitting the bench. Bo grasped her hand. "I'm so sorry. I wish you had felt that you could tell me. I would have been there for you."

"Would you? The man who used to laugh at any mention of me wanting a big family with the house, the yard and the swing set?"

He bowed his head. She had mentioned that swing set on many occasions. It had been on obsession of hers. An obsession that he had dismissed with a laugh. Because how else to deflect that which he'd once believed he hadn't any right to be a part of?

"It doesn't matter now," she said. "It was six years ago. From the moment I left my parents' place and moved to Paris, I focused on my work. And look where's it's gotten me."

"The boss lady."

"The boss lady." She squeezed his hand. "Though I am sorry for how I left you. At the time, I did owe you a reason for leaving. I shouldn't have done it that way. I reacted. I didn't know what else to do. The stay with my dad was good for me. It helped to clear my thoughts so I could put a plan together for my future. And Europe has always been my love, my dream. So I moved to Paris. Then I got to work."

That confession was not what he had expected to hear from her. Unable to have a child? Heavy stuff. He did wish she would have trusted him to tell him instead of running away. But at least he knew now.

The two of them had really changed directions over the years.

Did it bother Kiara that he had Emily? It

must. It shouldn't. It might. Bloody hell. But he wasn't sure how to ask about it, and he probably shouldn't. Anything to do with babies had to be a tender subject for her. Now he knew why she'd been keeping her distance from Emily.

"Thank you for sharing that with me," he whispered. "But you have to know that I'm here for you. Whatever you need. Just ask."

"That's sweet of you, Bo. But I'm actually fine now. I've shoved that devastating medical diagnosis into a closet and locked it tight. I rarely think about it. Well, that is until I walked into Emily's nursery."

"Sorry about that. I should have warned you."

"You had no way of knowing. And I should have been following your socials so I could have come to you with more knowledge of how your life has changed. I have learned a lot in the past few years. Number one is that I can take care of myself."

"I know that you can. But don't forget that sometimes it's nice to surrender and let others take care of things for you. You taught me that."

"How did I teach you that? Surrender is losing," she said. "Slow down? You lose. As a fighter who rarely loses a match, you must understand that."

"I'd never compare an MMA match to the misfortune life decided to hit you with. You taught me that life can be good. Different than what a man has been used to. That it can be right."

"Things were right for us. For a while." At her side, her phone buzzed. Kiara checked the screen. "Huh. I missed a call from my mom."

"Me and Chicken can start walking back. Give you some privacy?"

"No, it's okay. I'll call her when I get back to the chalet." She stood and dismissed the conversation as she wandered to the overlook to again snap some shots.

Life had smacked Kiara hard. And Bo had not been there to help her to her feet. Damn. Now he had an answer to the *why* she'd left him. It took away some of the sting. He should share with her the reason he'd been so adamant about not being a father. She didn't know about his father's abuse.

But did it matter now? He must be the one thing she most despised. A man with a baby. Something she could never have.

CHAPTER SIX

KIARA HAD TOLD Bo why she'd fled their relationship. The main reason. But not the catalyst: the miscarriage. It wasn't important now. Their lives had changed drastically. She was focused on her career. Bo was, remarkably, focused on raising his family.

Time to move forward.

By evening, the photographer had gotten some great interior shots, and he'd managed to snap outdoor shots of the property just before the rain started. With plans to send the photos to Lyle, he fist-bumped Kiara and left in a race out to his car to avoid the rain.

The rain dampened plans to cook outside on the grill for dinner. Since it was getting late, Bo had asked Kiara to spend the night again. With a refusal on her tongue, she'd conceded when he had reminded her the only inn in town was noted for its hourly rentals. And the Egyptian sheets in his guest room were not to be over-looked.

She hadn't intended for a three-day adventure here in Switzerland—she was out of fresh clothing—but another night wouldn't hurt. And she didn't mind someone cooking for her. Admittedly, she hadn't honed her cooking or baking skills over the years. Why bother, when it was only for one person? Takeaway and a fast salad cobbled from the market near her apartment served well enough.

Bo had concocted an amazing salad with radishes, carrots, sprouts, peaches, seeds and a tangy vinegar dressing that had blown her mind. How had a scrappy fighter mastered such culinary skills?

While he cleaned up in the kitchen, Emily lay on a blanket on the floor, but four feet from where Kiara sat on the couch with her laptop. A baby gym sporting bright wooden shapes captivated the tyke.

The impulse to move to her knees, crawl over and enjoy the baby's explorations struck. It was what she'd always done when she had babysat. A role she'd taken beyond her teen years and into her adult life, always offering to sit for friends' children. Knowing it was perfect training for when the day came that she started a family. But she didn't move from the couch. She hadn't watched or touched a friend's baby for, well, six years. The thought that if she touched Emily it would break down her emotional armor, topple her control, was strong. It was difficult enough, as it was, to simply sit there without grabbing the baby and kissing her silly.

She noticed Bo had paused, dish towel in hand, and must have been taking her in, taking in Emily. How they interacted with one another. Making notes? Kiara quickly focused back on the laptop screen. She'd confessed her secret—most of it. He had to understand her reluctance to get close to his daughter.

An hour later, with Emily tucked in for the night, they sat on the couch before the window, a bowl of popcorn on the table and non-alcoholic beers in hand, watching the rain.

"Won't you miss fighting?" Kiara asked. Tucking up her legs, she settled into the corner of the couch.

"Probably. But I won't miss having my face beaten to a pulp."

"Please, the Heartbreaker never lets his opponents get that close."

Bo chuckled. "He did at one time. And I'm not saying I'm old, and maybe it's the sudden rush of dad hormones, but I have slowed down. Marty says he doesn't notice it, but I do. My retreat is a second slower. My roundhouse might not make the mark exactly. I used to be able to clock a bloke on the ear with my foot and in the next second deliver a liver punch that would lay him flat."

"Well, you've been busy learning how to do the dad thing. If you incorporate practice back into your free time you'll gain that second back in no time."

"Here's to free time. I've forgotten what that is." He lifted his beer bottle in a toast and she clinked hers against it in a dull *ting*.

Free time. Yes, what was that exactly? The part where she looked away from her business to loll about on a white sand beach, not giving a thought about her agents, if the clients were satisfied, when they'd score their next double-digit million-dollar listing—no. She couldn't imagine not thinking about that stuff. Free time was overrated. Free time was something...mothers shared with their children. And Katherine Kirk had never bothered to seek such bonding time.

Thoughts about her mother surprised her. Really, she had grown up knowing only what it was like to have a distant mother. Kiara had expected to be left alone after school and forgotten on more than many occasions and recitals. So why did it bother her to remember that now?

Katherine Kirk had scoffed at Kiara's dreams

of motherhood. Had she become that woman now? Was it such a terrible thing?

"Still." Bo set down the bottle and stretched both his arms across the back of the couch as he put up his feet on the table. "I don't need to fight anymore. Not for money. I've earned enough to survive. Comfortably. And that includes planning for Emily's future. College, wedding, all that jazz. And if I'm not getting the same release of anger from the fight anymore then why do it?"

"Exercise? Challenge? Competition? It's what you do, Bo."

"It's what I did."

"Sure, but there must be something you still love about it?"

"The competition was key. Motivated me to be stronger, better, faster. But…not so much anymore. I'm morphing into something different. And I like it."

The satisfaction in his tone told her all she needed to know. Bo really was pivoting into becoming a new man, with a whole new lifestyle. And it looked good on him. She would never tell him the black-and-white-striped jeans he wore clashed horribly with the bright yellow T-shirt decorated with a purple mehndi design. It worked on him. He was unpredictable, both in the ring and in real life. And that would never change.

"So tell me about your realty company," he said. "How'd you get to be such a boss lady?"

"The usual hard work. Connecting with the right people. For the first year after we..." She sighed. "You know. I was relentless in learning who were the right people to not only advance my career, but to make it look good. I wanted every step I took to be made with integrity. Who to know to get the prime real-estate showings. Bankers, financiers, artists, designers. I went to fancy parties. I didn't have much to begin with. I had to hide the tag on the expensive clothing I bought to fit in, then would return it the next day."

"And look at you now. Wearing those fancy red-heeled shoes and looking like a million dollars." His eyes glided slowly over her skin. Kiara's core tingled with muscle memory. The man just had a manner of touching her without even moving.

Catching herself from a ridiculous sigh, Kiara said, "I earned every inch of those heels." And her mother would be proud.

"It shows." The man could look at her as much as he liked. Basking in his attention felt... good. "You're confident. But still. You used to be more..."

She waited as he searched for the right description, unsure she really wanted to know how he'd once thought of her.

"Open," he finally said. "Relaxed. Not so controlled."

If he only knew that was the only word that kept her on the top: control.

"I'm relaxed." She splayed her hand down her body to indicate her sprawled form on his couch. If he could read her at all, he'd know she was also feeling some skin-tingling desire.

"Sure, but you hold yourself differently now. Not that it's bad or wrong. You're put-together and your chin is always high. You're confidant and proud."

"Seems like good attributes to have."

"Very good." He turned toward her, stretching an arm to place his hand on the cushion next to her thigh. He couldn't quite reach her, not without adjusting his position. "So…"

So much in that one uttered word. She felt the same, if the same meant a brewing sexual tension.

"So?" she returned. His eyes had darkened. Pupils widened.

"After all you've been through. And now I understand why you walked away from me. Still don't like it, but I can have empathy for your needing to split and sort out your life. What I'm wondering now is…" He leaned onto an elbow. Looked up at her with those pretty blue eyes that she agreed should never again see a blow from a fist. "Want to try again?"

Exactly her thoughts. And, yes, she was curious about jumping in and giving it another go. But, no, she would be diving into tempestuous waters. Waters brewed with their past and her lies to him. Not even lies, just hiding truths. Could she put everything behind her and move forward with Bo? Did she want to?

Her body was ready to go the moment her logic set it free.

"Kiara? You're thinking about it too much. Makes me believe I don't have a chance. I get it. I just got a little too close for your comfort. And, man, has your comfort zone changed."

It had. But she didn't like hearing it from him. So she'd become her mother. What was wrong with pursuing a career and wanting to be the best? It was a career model with which Bo was very familiar.

"You always have a chance, Bo. I don't like saying it like that, though. Makes me sound like I'm something that has to be won. Like you need to pick up a gauntlet and meet a challenge."

"Aren't you something that should be won?"

"I'm not sure if I should take that to mean I'm difficult or I'm a challenge?"

"Of the two of us? I'll wear the difficult crown. But you wear the challenge tiara. And only because you are a woman who deserves the best. And hell if I know if I'm worthy of even treading your shadow nowadays."

"Oh, Bo, don't say things like that. You are worthy of…" Someone so much more caring and loving than she could be. He had a tendency to slip into that unworthy persona, and she wanted to wrap her arms around him and hug it away. But she didn't want to be his mother, or protector. She wanted much more in her life. From a relationship. "Why do you do that?"

"Do what?"

"Act like you don't deserve to have everything life offers you."

He sighed heavily. Sat back and looked up at the ceiling. "You had your secret, Kiara. I have mine."

"You mean about being a baby daddy?"

He chuckled, but without any levity. "You know how I always avoided conversations about my dad and family?"

"Yes. You used to change the subject like a boxer dodging a punch. And when I wanted to talk about you not wanting to be a father, instead of dodging it, you literally left for New York."

"You wanted to talk when I had to leave. You

know that, Kiara. I did promise we'd talk when I got back."

"I'll give you that." But then, she'd run away. No chance to talk. It wouldn't have mattered, anyway. At that moment in time, she had felt as if her life had been shattered. "Is it about your dad? I picked up that your mom was in an abusive relationship with him. Was I right?"

"Kiara." Bo rubbed his hands together before him, then, with a resolute nod, he said, "Dad used to beat on both of us. The older I got, the smarter I tried to be, and put myself in between Mum and Dad. Eventually he just went right for me."

"Oh, Bo. I…" Her heart fluttered and dropped. Never could she have imagined… "Why didn't you tell me this when we were dating? That's terrible."

He shrugged. "It's not something a man talks about. Men don't get beaten on."

"But at the time you weren't a— Little boys shouldn't have to take punches from their dads. Bo, you know that wasn't right. Oh, my God, I feel…"

"Don't feel bad for my pain, Duck. I've grown up. The first punch in every fight I've ever fought? That was for dear old dad. And now? I don't need that punch anymore. I'm the survivor."

He most certainly was. And here she'd been bemoaning how terribly life had treated her. If anyone had suffered, it had been Bo. He hurt. And he'd never had the courage to tell her when they had dated. If he had…

No wonder he'd been dead set against being a father.

Kiara clasped his hand. "Thank you for telling me that. I thought we knew so much about one another when we were dating. We were so good together."

"We were. Though, that was the sex. We weren't big on conversations."

"We talked. I know things about you. Just not about your dad beating you."

"Again, not something a man talks about. I try every day not to be like him."

Bo wasn't an abusive man. He never had been. But he must have chased that image because it was all he knew. It was probably why he had difficulty dating for extended periods. What had it been about her that had changed him? Six months must have been a forever in his life.

He shrugged. "I like talking now. Just the two of us. Being honest with one another. Maybe it's because I've been cooped up with Emily for months and have literally been talking to a pair of big blue eyes that can't talk back to me.

Well, she burbles. That's freakin' cute. Oi, I'm a nutcase, aren't I? I crave adult conversation. Connection."

He tapped her thigh. It was a little touch, but it succeeded in shocking an erotic thrill through her so-ready-for-anything system. "Do you think we might have a chance at…something?"

"Anything is always possible. We've learned a lot about one another today. Things we probably should have shared long ago. Maybe…do you think, knowing what we know now, would have changed things then?"

"Who can know? I think life happens exactly as it is supposed to happen. Maybe we weren't right for one another six years ago. But now? You were the one who kissed me by the pool," he said.

"I did because…" She frowned.

Where had she been going with that kiss? She hadn't a reason at the time beyond wanting to feel his mouth on hers. A test to see if he could still summon feelings in her. He had.

And she could relate to his wanting a connection. She conversed all the time with adults, but to really connect with them on a level beyond business? Should a single male client ever put out sensual vibes, her defense shields went up and she remained the consummate CEO.

Yet those shields were not activated at the moment.

"Doesn't matter your reason," he said. "I just want another one of those tasty kisses. Pretty please, Duck?"

It was crazy that his insistence on using that silly nickname for her actually turned her on. It was an intimate moniker that only they shared. His claim to her.

At that moment, a streak of lightning brightened the sky. Bo's jaw dropped and he cast her such a big-eyed gasp of wonder, Kiara giggled. And the emergence of a sound she had not indulged in forever loosened her posture. Sliding forward, she put her head close to his.

"Let's make out," she said.

"Thought you'd never ask."

With a move that could only be accomplished by a skilled martial arts fighter, Bo gently flipped Kiara to her back and pinned down her wrist. He hovered above her momentarily before hugging against her with his body and kissing down her neck. The heat of his mouth on her skin brought out shivers over her entire body. She wrapped her legs about his hips and coaxed his groin against hers. Mm, he was already hard. She didn't even consider the implications of her tease as she grinded her hips against his.

"You always get right to the point," he whispered as he trailed kisses from her earlobe to her jaw and then landed on her mouth with an insistent, deep splash inside her.

Her fingers raked through his soft hair, holding him there, telling him to never stop. Devour her. Make her his. It was something she'd not felt in so long. Even the men she'd briefly hooked up with over the years hadn't the ability to so instantly connect with her erotic zones and brew them to a wanting simmer.

When his hand glided down her dress, her nipples peaked to attention. She arched her back against his chest. Spreading her hands up his back, she felt the hard, taut deltoid muscles through the thin shirt. They undulated with his movements. The symphony of his body flowed against hers in a manner that felt so right. His hardness against her lithe softness. He covered her whole body with his and she felt safe and...

The word *loved* popped into Kiara's head. Not an accurate thought. More hopeful. Or was it desperate?

Hell, now she was thinking too much. She bracketed his face and parted their kiss.

Beautiful eyes glided between hers. This was too fast. *Was it?*

Kiara inched up from his confining clutch, putting her hands against his chest. His hard pecs pulsed rhythmically beneath her palms. *Oh, baby.* "Bo, don't do that. You're so silly."

"Just trying to show you my action, Duck." His left pec pulsed twice. "You want a piece of this?"

She did. And she didn't. "Please don't hate me but..."

His jaw dropped open. Defeat hazed his eyes.

"It just doesn't feel right at this moment," she said hastily. "It would be fast and furious."

"We do fast and furious well. Like old times."

"I agree, but we're not the same people anymore."

He bowed his head to her chest briefly, then sat back, knees to either side of her hips, and scratched the back of his head. "No, we certainly are not. You're right. Time to rein it in and act like the grown-ups we've become."

The disappointment in his tone hurt her to the very core. Kiara descended from the heady high of lusty contact with a crash. She closed her eyes. Why did she have to be a grown-up all the time? Couldn't she set aside the adult, smart, confident businesswoman for a few moments and just...enjoy life?

Be happy? *You are happy!*

Was she, though?

Bo stood and adjusted his striped jeans. They'd tightened to hug his erection. He had obviously felt the desire as well. "We headed to France tomorrow?"

"Yes."

"Then I need to catch some z's. We'll have to leave here by seven to catch the flight, and then to drop Emily at grandma's house. See you in the morning."

He strolled out of the room, leaving Kiara breathing heavily on the couch. She swore under her breath. That had not ended well. She was no longer the fun-loving Kiara who had fallen deeply for the electric, goofy, sensual fighter. But that woman was still inside. Somewhere.

Nor was Bo the charmer who could make her come with a glance. Well. He had gotten close. Too close. And he had confessed a deep dark secret to her, which had taken trust. He trusted her. Yet for some reason she was still pushing him away. Of the two of them, he had more reason to walk a wide circle around her. The one woman who could never step into his life. Because whichever woman he did end up with would ultimately become his daughter's mother.

And that thought broke Kiara's heart.

CHAPTER SEVEN

THE THREESOME FLEW to Charles de Gaulle Airport, outside of Paris, then parted ways. The viewings weren't until tomorrow. Bo drove to his mother's to drop off Emily. He'd invited Kiara along, but she'd made the excuse that she had work to do in Paris.

Really, she had only just met the baby. Did Bo expect her to step in and meet the grandmother as well? It was hard enough to not grab Emily and snuggle her and drown her in kisses. She hadn't touched her yet. Didn't dare. How could she? It was like watching a lottery winner flaunt his winnings while she stood there with an empty wallet. Did Bo not get that?

Yet, she'd left out the most important part when she'd confessed to him. And that was too much to think about, or risk, right now. Because she needed to keep this client. If the media learned Bowen James hadn't gotten along with the Queen of Luxury Real Estate and had fired her? Kirk Prestige Homes did not need that bad press.

So after a too-brief kiss goodbye from Bo, Kiara took a cab to her Paris apartment. Because: change of clothes. Paperwork with Lyle. Phone calls to make. Even though she was focused on selling Bo's place right now, that didn't mean all the other details fell to the wayside. She had sold a property in Marseille last week and Lyle texted to say he'd meet her with the closing documents.

She hadn't established an office for Kirk Prestige Homes. The other two agents worked remotely, and it was an efficient business model. But the need for a central location to have the occasional in-person meeting, keep supplies and hold client presentations was next on her list. She'd assigned Lyle the task of scouting locations in Paris. Nothing too fancy, but not minuscule, either. They needed to present a luxurious facade without breaking the bank for a place that may only be used a few times a month by any of the agents.

After ending her call to her mom, Kiara tucked her phone away in her bag. It had forwarded to messages again. If anyone was busier than Kiara it was her sixty-two-year-old mother, who never paused for a break. Katherine Kirk had made a name for herself in New York as the go-to woman for venture capital for female-run businesses. She loved building up other women, and that business acumen had rubbed off on Kiara.

As well, the need to prove herself to her mother, in any way, was always there. Kiara couldn't recall the last time she'd gotten a hug from her mom. So approval for her business success was the next best thing.

True to his word, Lyle was walking down the Rue de l'échelle as the cab dropped her off. The man's timing was impeccable. He might take off more days than necessary, but when in work mode he was there two hundred percent. And he had recently gotten married to his partner of three years, so he was all about finding them a lovers' nest to begin a family.

Between the two of them, they'd shared their personal stories and had developed a friendship and trust that went beyond a mere business relationship. Kiara was glad for it. Her friendships were rare and few. Her best friend, Viviane, had recently fallen in love with a jeweler right here in Paris, but somehow she made the relationship work even as Viv traveled Europe for her gardening business. Kiara made a mental note to text her to find out when next she'd land in Paris so they could meet for lunch.

Lyle waved as he got nearer and smooched an air kiss at her.

"*Cherie*!" Lyle gave the best bear hugs and he managed to work one in despite an armload of files, a laptop and his ever-present latte. "You look…tired?"

Kiara ignored that comment as she punched in the digital code for her building. She walked through a heavy iron doorway and down a spacious, tiled hallway that opened into a circular open-air courtyard with a modest crop of shrubbery and white irises in the center. She lived on the fifth floor, and the elevator only fit one.

"It's called working hard," she muttered as she stepped into the elevator and waved at Lyle. "Meet you up top."

At her floor, she rolled her stuff out and into her apartment. The small domicile had two and a quarter rooms. The kitchen and living area were one. The bedroom held a twin bed and a clothes rack. And the bathroom was set into the edge of the roof, allowing only for a person to stoop to actually sit on the toilet.

She did not consider this place home. Kiara Kirk didn't have a home. Her job was to find homes for others. And really, she was never here. The rent was astronomical. She was just fortunate to have nabbed the property, half a block from the Louvre in the trendy first arrondissement, when it had come on the market. Location, location, location!

Leaving her suitcase and bags by the kitchen counter—no table…no room—she sat on the love seat and then turned her body and collapsed, calves dangling over the arm.

Lyle stepped inside while slurping the dregs of his latte and aimed for the floor in front of the love seat. He knew the drill. His apartment was the same size as hers. And he had a husband with whom he shared that tiny space.

"After you sell the MMA fighter's place you need to help me and Remy find our home."

"Really?" Smiling, she closed her eyes, too content to sit up, and needing the rest after the emotional roller coaster of the past few days. "I'd be happy to. What's your price range?"

Lyle sighed heavily.

Yes, she knew it wasn't even in range of the cheapest homes she sold. Generally, her properties were from five to ten million. That was standard. The most expensive she'd sold was a sixty-million-euro chateau in Marseille. That commission had kick-started her decision to treat herself with a new pair of shoes to celebrate each sale. A dozen pairs were currently holding a place of honor tucked in boxes beneath the narrow bed.

"I'll do it," she said. "But I might have to search some of the lower-priced offerings."

"Please do. As low as you can go. Remy may be a lawyer but he's still paying off college. That idiot decided to go to school in the States instead of here, where it's nearly half the price. No matter. He's adorable, so I forgive him. I think we want something in the fifth."

"Touristy."

"Yes, but close to the park and—"

"Never in your price range, sweetie. Sorry."

"I know." His shoulders slumped. "A guy can dream, right?"

"Always. But maybe I can find something in the fourteenth? It touches the fifth and does offer some newer, but smaller apartments. Anyway, what do we have to be verified, signed and notarized?"

"Lots." He opened a briefcase and pulled out a stack of papers, most clipped off with a variety of colored clips. Lyle's organization skills were off the charts. "How long are you in Paris?"

"Just today. As you know, I show Mr. James a couple homes tomorrow. I needed this stopover to do a clothing change and…" Not think about the sexy man she'd made out with last night.

"Well, well, well." Lyle leaned back on his palms. He had a certain smirk that was more of a smile, but also brimmed with teasing wonder. "Mr. James, eh? So formal. Was it good seeing the old boyfriend again? Did he introduce you to his erm…baby?"

"He did."

"And?" The anticipation in his voice was obvious. "Are you okay?"

"I survived." Lyle was aware of her medical condition. "Didn't hold her, though. Didn't dare. Bo is currently dropping her off at Grandma's so we can look at houses without toting along a diaper bag and bottles." Kiara rolled to her side and her face was right next to Lyle's genuinely concerned mug. "She's the most adorable baby I've ever seen."

"Oh, *cherie*, it'll be okay."

"Promise?"

He sighed and sorted some of the papers into piles on the floor before him. "I'd never lie to you."

"You're a good man, Lyle. And so is Bo. He's turned into a wonderful father."

"Sexy."

"Really?" She put up a palm. "No, don't even

go there. I know you and Remy have been filling out adoption forms. The whole world is baby crazy, and here I am…"

"Listen, girlfriend, I know how you hurt, and that is your right. I'm not going to tell you how to live or handle the tough things life tosses your way. But I'm also not going to let you wallow in something you can't change. Just know, when Remy and I do finally get to adopt, you are going to be the official godmother-slash-aunt to that urchin."

"And I will proudly wear that tiara."

"I'm the only one who gets to wear the tiara." He winked.

Kiara laughed. And for the rest of the afternoon, they ordered in food and got a lot of work done.

Emily had the most amazing giggle. It birthed in her belly and was thunderously cute. Bo blew raspberries on her stomach while his mother prepared lunch. As a former seamstress who once worked for Dior in London, she'd not stopped sewing even after retirement. When they'd arrived with a spit-up emergency, Mum had changed out the soiled onesie for a little blue sundress with yellow chickens on it. And sewn in script along the neckline was the word *Heartbreaker.*

"You're my little heartbreaker." Bo delivered another raspberry to Emily's tummy. "Even Grandma knows that."

"I think she's actually a heart mender." His mother cut off the edges the cheese-and-ham sandwich and arranged it on a plate with crisps and a vinegar potato salad. "She makes my heart feel full. I'm so happy to have her stay with me, Bo."

"Yeah, but Daddy will miss you," he said to Emily, who gripped his hair and tugged. "So strong! She's going to be a fighter like Daddy."

"Heaven forbid," his mum said.

And that uncensored bit of truth brought the light mood to a halt. Bo placed Emily in the high chair while battling with the image how he'd perfected his dodge only because he'd been forced to by a drunk father. Once he'd hit his teen years, his mother had started saying it to him—*Don't be like your father.*

So what had he grown up to do? Well, he had avoided alcohol and gambling. But it was the carousel of women that would brand him as his dad. And that swift right hook. Bo winced to recall the times he hadn't dodged fast enough and had caught that hook against his shoulder, body or a temple.

No way did he wish his daughter would grow up to be like her dad.

"Right, you're going to be a princess who rides a unicorn and saves the world with kindness," he told Emily.

She smacked a palm into the carrots his mother had prepared for her. A splat of carrot hit him in the eye.

"She does have a great right hook, though," he commented. "Are those carrots organic?" He grabbed half the sandwich and took a bite. Oh, yes, lots of spicy mustard.

"They are from my garden, Bowen. Of course, they are organic."

Good ol' Mum, always looking after his daughter. It made Bo wince to recall what she had gone through with his father. Once Bo had started taking the blows from his dad, they'd lessened for his mother. They'd never discussed the abuse. And he didn't know how to bring it up. It was too late now. Killian James had died eight years earlier. Bo was determined to make his daughter's life one-hundred-percent different than his childhood had been.

"Now—" his mum waved a mustard-laden knife before her "—talk to me about the Realtor. Can she sell your house? Will she find you a new home close to me? Did the woman who broke my son's heart apologize?"

That last question was delivered with the sharp tone his mother reserved for those she was suspicious about. And a splat of mustard onto the countertop. Madeline James did not hate, but she could serve a nasty stink eye and ignore you until you begged for mercy.

"She explained her reason for ghosting me."

"Which was?"

"Kiara found out she couldn't have children."

"Oh. That's awful." Tutting in sympathy, she poured herself some lemonade and put the pitcher back in the fridge. When she turned back to him, she tilted her head curiously. "I wonder how she found that out. She had to have been tested, or in the process of seeking an answer for the condition. When did that happen? You two were dating then. Did you know she was going through that?"

"Hadn't a clue."

"Yes, but still. Curious that she would suddenly learn something like that while dating you. I wonder…"

Bo set down the sandwich. "Wonder what, Mum?"

"Huh? Oh, nothing. It's over between you two. So no worries."

"I would never call what Kiara and I have over."

His mom picked up the knife again and this time her gesture felt a little too threatening. "Bo, you be careful around her. That woman toyed with your heart."

"Thanks, Mum." With a careful touch to her wrist, he directed the knife down to the countertop. "But there's already a girl toying with my heart." He leaned over and kissed Emily's carrot-covered nose. "And she can do whatever she wants with it. I love you, Chicken. Only a couple days and Daddy will be back for you again. Hopefully I can find a house in that time. Kiara's a pro. She'll make it happen."

"You can leave Emily here as long as it takes," his mum said. "It's nice having a little one in the house."

"Did you get the delivery?" Bo had supplies delivered a week ago in anticipation that he might need to utilize his mum as a babysitter during the house-hunting adventure.

"Yes, the crib is beautiful and so is the rocking chair. But I'm not sure what the electronic thingy is for."

"It's a sleep soother. It plays heartbeat sounds

to comfort her. Like being in her mum's womb. She loves it."

"Emily needs a real mother's heartbeat, Bo."

"Mum."

His mother shrugged. "I'm just saying. You've done an amazing job with her. I'm so proud of you, Bo. But someday, you'll want your daughter to have some feminine influence in her life."

He agreed. But when or how would he know who the right person would be for Emily? Dare he consider it might be Kiara?

CHAPTER EIGHT

BO KNOCKED ON Kiara's apartment door. He'd managed to slip inside the locked building entrance by smiling at an elderly woman as she'd been leaving.

The door opened to Kiara's surprised expression.

He held out the flowers. "I had planned to stay overnight with Mum and Emily, but then I saw the pile of clothes in the laundry room and noticed the guest room was stacked with assorted piles of junk so I let her off the hostess hook. She has her hands full."

Kiara took the roses and breathed in their scent.

"There are only eleven," he said. "Had to bribe one of your neighbors to get inside."

"Clever. Come in. I just surfaced from piles of paperwork and realized it's almost dark out. I was thinking about ordering take away. How does coq au vin from the restaurant down the street sound?"

"Like much-needed protein." He took in the small living area combined with the half kitchen. More like an idea of a kitchen. These Paris apartments were always tiny. "Good thing I booked a room at the Hotel Regina. It's just down the street. Makes me feel like a king when I stay there."

"I do love their beaux arts decor. So luxurious."

"I'll grant that this place is prime real estate." Bo closed the door behind him and wandered inside. "But what is a boss lady who sells million-dollar homes doing living in this supply closet?"

He bent to peer out the narrow window that overlooked the courtyard. It was a beautiful day and the window was open to allow in the sultry evening heat. No bug screens, just curtains. He did love Paris.

"It's basically a stopover. A place to regroup after a long flight." She put the roses in a large glass and fluffed them. "I live in hotel rooms. I've gotten used to room service and finding mints on my pillow. Not to mention massages on request, designer-clothing delivery and front-row tickets to the hottest shows."

"Brilliant. But wouldn't you rather have a

home to call your own instead of always looking for others?"

She shrugged and sorted through the papers spread out on the living room floor, gathering them into a neat stack and gesturing that Bo sit on the tiny couch. "Some day. When I slow down."

"Let me guess. That's never?" Because he knew slowing down to her meant taking the time to have a family. And what he now knew...

"Oh, I intend to slow my pace. I'm interviewing another agent next week. Hope to bring her onto my team to make four agents. With more team members, I can start taking the occasional day off."

"A day?" He plopped onto the couch. It was surprisingly comfy, though the decorative gold fringy stuff bordering the edges looked like something he could easily ruin. "Is it worth it?"

She slid onto the one barstool by the short kitchen counter, sliding up a leg to tuck under her other bent leg. She wore soft blue yoga pants and a T-shirt that was cut low. She looked so comfortable. Bo guessed it was a look she would never allow the rest of the world to see. Boss lady relaxed.

"Is what worth what? Working all the time?" She ruffled her fingers through her curly hair. The move worked like a touch down Bo's neck, igniting his senses to ultra-alert. "I think so. I'm building a nest egg."

"Nothing wrong with having an egg filled with cash. But…"

Did she not see how utterly alone she was? What had happened to the real Kiara Kirk? Her life had taken such a dramatic turn. It hurt Bo's heart to know he hadn't been allowed to help her through the one time when she had most needed a shoulder to cry on.

"What do you care?" Kiara said. "You should be thankful for my focus on business. I'll get you the most for your property and find you the best deal on your new home. And finding homes for celebrities gives the agency more exposure. It makes me happy."

"Really? I remember when the dream of family was the only thing you believed could bring you happiness."

"I was wrong."

A curt response. He'd touched a nerve, but he wasn't willing to back off. Not when really needing to understand the woman felt important to him. Because he'd not taken the time to understand her six years ago. So now…

"You weren't wrong. You just got bad news, Kiara. About not being able to have a family… at least not the 'regular' way. It can happen. There's always—"

"Let's not talk about the things that changed our lives for the worse this evening, okay?"

"Why not? I'm interested in all of you, Kiara. It's important to me to get to know you again."

Had she realized she'd said *for the worse*? So she wasn't happy. And that was clear to him.

"I appreciate that, I really do, but…" She blew out a breath. "I'm tired after hours of paperwork. Can we just order food and chill?"

Bo picked up on her signal to drop it, so he'd checked himself.

"Sounds like a date to me. You order the food and I'll run out and get it. Then we'll snuggle until we fall asleep."

When he expected her to protest or remind him about his hotel reservation, she instead grabbed her phone and put in an order to the restaurant.

Now, to play this cool, but not too cool. He was sitting in a tiny apartment with the one woman he'd fallen madly for years ago. And since she'd stepped through the door of his chalet all those old feelings had resurfaced and were nudging him to make a move. Tell her how he felt. But not in the wrong way. Kiara was a runner. He didn't want her to run again. It was important to get their ground rules straight before diving in again.

As well, his mother's question about how

Kiara found out she couldn't have children bothered him. He wanted Kiara to explain, but knew
there was a right and a wrong time for that talk.
And she'd made it clear tonight was not right.

Tonight, Bo decided, was for getting to know
one another beyond business.

The coq au vin was accompanied by a spiced
berry compote heaped with fresh blueberries.
Taking the dessert to the love seat, Kiara and
Bo sat beside one another. Bo had started the
play by tossing a berry into the air and catching
it in his mouth. She matched his move. When
he started tossing them at her, and she miracu-
lously caught each one, the competition ensued.

"Five!" Kiara declared victoriously as she
chewed another blueberry.

Bo's thigh brushed alongside hers. His shoulder rubbed hers with every movement. And
his body heat soaked through her clothing and
melted into her skin like a hot summer day.
Every part of her was aware of every part of
him. She had almost missed that last attempt
because it was growing harder to concentrate
on the game when the man she'd like to tackle
seemed so oblivious to her growing desire. Or
was he?

"Tie," Bo said. "And there's two left. I say we
both toss at the same time. Winner takes all."

"Sounds logistically complicated, but…" She snapped her neck and rolled her shoulders. "Let's do it!"

The simultaneous toss resulted in Bo slipping to the right, the blueberry beaning him between the eyes. Kiara snapped for the prize and caught it, her forehead bumping his as she did so.

"Seriously?" Bo clutched his forehead. "You've got a hard head, Duck."

"Oh, come on, that was just a nudge. Does the big, tough MMA fighter want to cry?" She opened her mouth to teasingly display the blueberry.

"Yeah? I'll show you how a real fighter wins his match."

He dove in for a kiss, his lips opening hers and his tongue dashing in deeply. It was a sneaky move, one that was as much a part of the game as she expected. When Bo snagged the prize and parted from her, she shoved him playfully.

"Cheater!"

He chewed the blueberry he'd stolen from her mouth. "More like winner. Now what's my prize?"

"You just got it. I hope you enjoyed that blueberry."

"Not as much as I enjoy kissing you."

With a tug, he pulled her to his chest and

their mouths magnetically joined. So she hadn't fought the move. Sue her. Bo tasted like blueberries and the wine they'd had with dinner. And of losing herself in something so wondrous she might never resurface. The real world could continue without her. Her agents could take over the agency. And she could be happy.

He parted the kiss and she pressed her forehead to his. "I missed your presence," he said.

As had she. "I missed your laugh."

"Feels like old times. Want to make love, Duck?"

Kiara leaned back. Her legs were entangled with his. Her shirt was pushed up. Her hair was tangled in her lashes. Exhilaration shimmered across her skin. And Bo's gleaming blue eyes defied her to resist his invitation. She did want sex, in the greater sense that it had been months since she'd hooked up with a man. She needed that closeness, that sensual treat, the release. Hell, the orgasm.

But what if they did have sex now? Then they went to view homes tomorrow. Bo found one he liked. Bought it. They might have sex a few more times. But ultimately, that would be the end of it. Because she couldn't imagine a future with Bo *and* Emily. It didn't feel like something she was allowed to have. And who was she to think she could march into the man's life and assimilate into the bliss he was currently creating for himself and his daughter?

"Duck?" He rapped her skull gently with his knuckles. "You're thinking too hard again. You never used to do that. You used to dive in and take life by the balls."

"You said yourself I've changed. We have to be realistic about things, Bo."

"Having sex requires a major think?"

"It requires we know exactly what we're getting into."

"Right. You don't want to have sex with me because I have a kid and I'm not the man you used to know."

He was…so close.

"And I shouldn't have sex with you," he continued, "because you broke my heart and now you're some ice queen who will walk out of my life the moment you've had your way with me."

Kiara pushed out of the embrace and paced to the kitchen counter. That statement had been entirely uncalled for.

And yet, was he right?

"I think I put that the wrong way," he said.

"You think?" She turned on him. "Who is using who for sex here, Bo? Because it's not me. You were the one to suggest it."

"I suggested it because I like getting naked with you, Kiara. And I thought we were having a moment. And you liked having sex with me, too. Don't deny it."

"Of course, I like having sex with you. You were the best lover I've ever had!"

"Then why are we yelling all these nice things at each other like we're arguing? It seems like we should be focusing that energy into something more pleasurable."

Why indeed? Sometimes the man could bring her back to reality with the plainest of truths. She loved that about him.

Screw their past. Live in the moment. If only, for the moment she had with him.

Kiara crossed the room and grabbed Bo by the shirt. "Come on."

He followed her into the bedroom, remarked on the hobbit-sized twin bed, then dutifully sat on that tiny bed when she shoved him down.

"You want to have sex?" she asked, hands to her hips. "So do I. And whatever happens afterward, we promise to be adults and just handle it. Agreed?"

"Those are your terms?"

"Those are my terms."

Bo held up his fist for her to bump. "Deal."

They fell into lovemaking as if they'd never stopped touching one another so many years ago. Feeling one another's skin. Tasting one another's mouths. Touching spots that stirred shivers. Lingering in spots that made their bodies quake. Knowing when to pause, when to speed up, when to meet one another's gazes.

Kiara looked down at Bo's Popsicle-colored eyes. Neon lights from outside shone across the bed. He smiled at her and closed his eyes as she rocked on top of him, building up the pressure, taking him to an edge that she knew to lead him to. He followed. Gripping the bedsheets with his hands, he surrendered control to her. And she took it.

It was what she did best.

When his body shook below her and his hands gripped her ankles, she felt him overcome. The power of his release gave her such pleasure. And the movement of his body against her pushed her over that same edge.

They came together. Breathy gasps and clawing fingernails. She tilted back her head, feeling the cool breeze from the open window whisper across her breasts.

No regrets, she decided. No matter what happened between the two of them. And that meant she must make this moment last forever. Because it was not something she ever wanted to lose.

What felt like hours later, the twosome were lying on the bed, Bo hugging Kiara from behind, not so much to extend the lovemaking but because if he let go she may fall off the narrow bed.

The bedroom was placed so perfectly that a person could see the flash of the lights at the very peak of the Eiffel Tower from here. If they tilted their head just right. And squinted.

Still. It was strangely romantic.

Nuzzling his nose aside her neck, Bo kissed her lightly. Here. There. She was so blissed out, it didn't matter where he touched her—it now felt less like a sensual trigger and more reassuring and as if they were one entity.

"This feels right," he said.

It did. But she wasn't prepared to admit to that. Not when it felt so easy. Life was never this easy. She had to brace for the smack. Because that was also part of life. The smackdown.

"Paris does that to a person," she said. "Makes life feel a little more magical than reality. Also, good sex and the high we're both on? It's like a drug, Bo. Just don't think too much now." She slid a hand down his stomach. "Want to go again?"

Bo laughed and rolled over on top of her, moving with as much energy and enthusiasm as the world-famous Heartbreaker he was known for being in the ring. But this was no fight.

This could be the beginning of something new.

But Bowen could never be the missing piece

to her puzzle. He'd found his family and was moving forward to something new and wondrous. Kiara couldn't control him, and she didn't want to. That fact made having sex with him a safe bet for Kiara. A condom wrapper was lying on the floor. The chances of her getting pregnant were astronomical. But could it happen? She wasn't sure she could handle that blow again.

And yet, just now she realized something. When life hadn't given her what she wanted, she had decided to control life. Had leaving Bo been her way to control *him*? By denying him information about what had really happened to her was she continuing to control him? Just like her mother would have done?

Katherine Kirk would be so proud.

So why did Kiara feel a revolting lump rise in her throat?

CHAPTER NINE

SINCE THE PLEDGE of Kirk Prestige Homes was to show the client an exemplary experience while they viewed properties, Kiara had rented a brand-new yellow Lamborghini convertible for the ride. Bo had insisted on driving. Fine with her. There was something about speeding down a paved country road with trees lining one side and a flowered meadow humming with bees on the other side.

Wind blowing through her hair, and radio blasting rock tunes, Kiara lifted her arms high and tossed back her head. "I love this!"

Bo chuckled and turned down the radio. "You really come alive in the fresh air. And did I tell you how beautiful you look today?"

"You did, a few times already. It's the air. I love driving fast and feeling free."

It wasn't often she got to figuratively let down her hair and slip into a loose dress and low heels. She'd decided against stilettos today because they'd be walking across land and probably through woods and rough surfaces. And she didn't need to impress Bo with a sexy dress anymore. Maybe. Well, she'd nixed the tight red number at the last minute and had gone with a slim-fitted dress that stopped midthigh with white lace trim. Red florals swept across a yellow background. Add in her pink lipstick, and a pink silk scarf tied at her neck? Summertime drenched her with anticipation.

And this was a great day to spend alongside a man who still had a grasp on her heart. And her libido. Oh, last night…. Truly, the two of them had been created for one another when it came to making love. Bo still remembered all her erotic zones, and she knew his. They'd fallen asleep somewhere around three in the morning, exhausted, elated and snuggled against one another in the subdued flashes of neon from the nearby Tuileries.

But she'd woken this morning with a curse upon hearing the clatter of the shower against the bathroom tiles. Bo was such an early riser. She'd hurried through her morning beauty routine, not wanting to keep him waiting. He'd threatened to curl his own hair if she took too long. So she had fluffed some loose curls and gone with minimal makeup. But she would never go without her lipstick.

The way Bo adored her with a lingering gaze? Didn't matter how she looked, as long as the one admiring her was him.

She knew she should be all business today, and she would be once she set foot on the property, but if a little flirtation slipped in here and there, she wasn't going to fight it.

"Just ahead," she said.

The GPS on her phone directed them to the first home that she had visited earlier this spring. It was at the high end of Bo's budget, and might be a bit much, with elaborate furnishings and decor, but it offered lots of land and a pool and tennis court. It also featured a vineyard. Of the two properties she would show him today, she suspected this might not be the one to win his heart. Always best to start with the number-two home instead of the winner.

"Is this the one close to Bear's place?" Bo asked as he navigated the drive toward the eighteenth-century mansion framed by a five-car garage on one side and a guesthouse on the other side.

"That's the next house. And as far as I can tell from the map, I believe your mom may be within half an hour of each."

"Excellent."

"How did your mother ever end up in France, anyway?" she asked as they got out of the car.

She grabbed the file from her briefcase, along with her phone.

Bo finished the water he'd brought and tucked the empty bottle back in the car. He smoothed a palm along the car's sunny yellow finish. She'd known he'd love the ride. And if that put him in an exemplary mood, then he'd be more open to today's viewings.

"It's where her boyfriend lives," he said.

"Madeline James has a boyfriend? That's great! It's great, right?"

If she remembered correctly, it had been about eight years since Bo's dad had passed away from cirrhosis.

"It's brilliant. Mum has never been happier, and she finally has a man who genuinely cares about her. And he's rich." He winked at her. "Had to arm-wrestle him last Christmas to see who would get to buy her the mustang she's always wanted. I won. Heh."

"What color?"

Bo strolled up beside her and put an arm around her shoulder as they approached the estate. "Not a car, Duck. Mum wanted a mustang horse. She rides it every day."

"Wow. But she doesn't bring Emily near it, does she?"

Bo regarded her with a squeeze of her shoulders. "Nope. But I love that that is where you went with the info."

She shrugged. "Baby-proofing is hard. But she's raised one awesome man, so I shouldn't have said anything."

"You can be honest with me, Kiara. About everything. I like it when you speak your mind."

She caught his sudden serious tone and looked away from his blue eyes. Whatever he'd implied, she didn't want to get into right now. She'd confessed about her medical condition. What more did he believe she wasn't telling him?

Was it really necessary that he know *all* the details?

There's that control again, Kiara. Do you really want to keep controlling the man with secrets? Focus.

Right. She had a house to sell. And a man who wanted to get back to his daughter. The quicker she could find Bo his dream home, the faster he returned to Emily and made sure his mother didn't bring her around a wild and reckless horse.

There was no lockbox on the front door. Kiara entered the digital code and pushed open the door. Bo strode inside and took in the vast, open three-story entry.

Switching into sell mode, Kiara rattled off

the square footage, the amenities, all the standard info, as they wandered the marble-tiled halls and into the kitchen, where Bo meticulously took in everything. He opened all the cupboards. Sat on the chairs. Opened the windows. Slid a hand along the pristine gray marble countertops.

Up on the second floor, he tested wherever the hardwood floor creaked. Pushed back curtains to better view the lush forest at the back of the property. And, like a discerning Goldilocks, he plopped onto each bed in the six bedrooms.

Kiara wandered across the master bedroom and flicked on the bathroom light switch. "All the furniture comes with this chateau," she said. "So if you like that bed, it's yours."

"It's kind of lumpy." He sat up and bounced a few times. "And did you notice all the beds have these creepy canopy things on them? It's so…"

"Medieval?"

"Yes." He jumped off the bed and strolled over to meet her in the bathroom, which, like the others, was lush with ornamental details and fusty gold, olive and maroon colors. "This whole place feels so…old for me. I mean, it's gorgeous. And certainly luxurious. A wine fridge *and* a beer fridge in the kitchen? Nice. But it's not me, Kiara. Do you actually think this place is me?"

"The furnishings? No. But I did think you'd like the garage and outdoor amenities. The pool and back patio area are like another home in itself. You could spend the whole day out there. There's even an outdoor kitchen with yet another fridge. And I know you like to cook and make smoothies."

"Sounds promising. Let's go check it out."

An hour later, they'd surveyed the garages and walked the property limits, and Bo had dipped his hand into the pool. Now they sprawled on the patio lounge chairs. The sun was high, so they found the electronic controls for the sun shade and rolled it out.

"What's the price?" Bo asked.

"Fifteen million."

"Above my budget."

"Not if I sell your place for eighteen. And you love the garage."

"I do. It would fit all my cars if I reduced the shop area to add in the Mini. And you're right about this outdoor setup. This is very nice. I could transform the guesthouse into a gym. That would be great. But…"

Kiara knew what that *but* meant. And she wasn't going to take it personally. It was client-speak for *I'm not too sure*.

"On to house number two?"

He reached out and took her hand in his. "I appreciate you doing this for me, Kiara."

"Appreciation isn't necessary. I do get a commission. A healthy one."

"I know, but you know. You taking a chance on coming back into my life."

She squeezed his hand. "I wanted to. And I'm glad I did."

"It's because of the sex, right? We do rock the world together."

"We do. But that's not why I'm glad I agreed to this. You're doing well, Bo. I'm very happy for you. And even though a baby was probably the last thing you would have ever wished for, it seems like Emily has had a positive effect on you. You have it all."

"I'm glad you see that. But I don't have everything. I still need the perfect home. And…"

"And?"

He shrugged, then offered nonchalantly, "I've decided I want you back in my life."

"Have you?" The announcement didn't surprise her so much as make her inner dreamer sit up and clap. But she wasn't that daydreaming woman anymore. At least, she had strived not to be. It was difficult not to relax and sink into the former Kiara, into the swing set and picket fence fantasies, when around Bo. He made life feel so easy. "Cheeky of you."

"That's not cheeky. This is." He slid off the chair and moved over to take her in his arms.

His kisses were never routine or the same. Each one told her something different and touched her in a way she'd never thought possible. This kiss recognized her with an ease and urgency. It fluttered at the crown of her head and went down her neck, where his fingers softly stroked, and then shimmied down her spine to tickle in her core with promises of oh, so delicious sex.

When he parted from the kiss, Kiara sighed and said heavily, "Well."

"Well?" he asked. "What do you think about my plan to win you back? Do I have a chance?"

Did he? Yes!

No.

Hell, yes, he did. But by stepping back into Bo's life she was stepping into someone else's life. Emily's. And Kiara wasn't sure how that would work for her wounded heart. Did she even have a right to step into the mom role with another woman's baby? To have something she wasn't allowed to have?

"Kiara, tell me you want to try again. You like having sex with me."

"I do."

"You like spending time with me doing things that don't involve us getting naked."

"I do."

"You like a lot of things about me. In fact, I would propose that you like everything about me. The only reason you broke it off was because you got scared. Freaked out. And I'm not making light of it. I really wish I could have been there for you when you found out about that terrible thing. I would have been there for you."

"I believe that you would. And, yes, I freaked out, and should have been honest with you at the time. But it's in the past now, Bo. Let's move forward."

"Like, trying-again forward?"

"You are very insistent."

"I'm a fighter. No matter what you toss at me I keep bouncing back, slipping into all my angles, keeping you in check. Is it working?"

She nodded. "Let's see what happens."

"That's not a definitive yes, but I'll take it. I'd kiss you again, but I just noticed the security camera above the door over there."

"Oh, hell." Kiara sat up and fluffed her fingers through her hair. "I forgot about those. They're all over the house. Okay, let's lock this place up and on to the next property."

"If we drive through a town on the way, we're going to do lunch first."

"Deal."

* * *

It wasn't a town, but rather a quaint village with stone houses and a herd of goats standing roadside that Bo had to whistle at. A shop sold fresh sandwiches, jars of home-canned dill pickles and mint lemonade. With their booty spread on a tea towel that sported a list of French wines, they picnicked on a bench by a pond that boasted a pair of white swans with frilly tail feathers.

The day felt idyllic. And that Kiara had not refused Bo when he'd told her he wanted to pursue her had made his day. More enthusiasm would have been preferable. But he did understand that she was in business mode today. And he appreciated that, but only when they were touring a house.

So what had happened to his rule about not letting her back into his heart?

Weren't rules made to be broken? She'd told him why she'd ghosted him. He'd confessed about his difficult childhood. Now the table was clear and they could move forward. He'd like that. He enjoyed making love with Kiara. So his rule regarding not allowing her back into his heart had to bend, at least a little. He wasn't sure how he wanted this all to go, but right now, he intended on enjoying being with her.

Now, as they tossed their refuse in the bin

outside the market and wandered back to the car, he followed Kiara's sexy walk. Even in flat soles, those hips of hers spoke loudly. They demanded he dance with her. And he wasn't a dancer. That had been proven when he'd done *a reality dancing competition* and had been the third star out; he'd not even made it to the semifinals. Attempting the cha-cha had only discombobulated his usual fluid martial-arts movements. But he did have some moves between the sheets.

He'd been tempted to try out those moves back at the first house on the patio. Good thing he'd noticed the camera. The last thing he needed was a tape of he and Kiara showing up on social media. Since Emily had entered his life, he strived for privacy. He would no longer consider a reality-television appearance that required he walk naked through a forest or smooch an unknown woman in the dark.

Who was that man who had done that stuff? Forlorn. Seeking. Heartbroken. He'd sought validation after Kiara's departure from his life. Because it had felt like a punch from his dad, one of those sneaky jabs he hadn't seen coming until it was too late. And he'd found some validation before the eyes of millions of viewers and in the comments and likes of social media.

But such surface admiration had grown stale.

And while it would take some doing, by announcing his retirement, he felt the paparazzi would soon find other celebrities to stake out and annoy. He was pulling down his shingle.

When Kiara leaned over the car door to grab her files from the seat, Bo hustled over and slid a hand along her thigh and hip. He leaned over her, and as she stood, he straightened with her. She melted against his chest and tilted back her head. Her lush, thick hair tickled his neck and chin.

"You always smell like sunshine and fruit," he murmured as he kissed below her earlobe. "And you taste even better."

She turned and pulled him down by his shirtfront for a long, deep kiss. Now this was what he liked most about her. She was never afraid to take what she wanted.

Could a man's heart dance? Bo was pretty sure his did as Kiara's mouth crushed his. They didn't need to cha-cha—they performed moves of their own.

"You taste like a pickle sandwich," she said. "We only have until six at the next place, so that gives us four hours. Probably better hustle."

"You think we'll need that much time there?"

"You never know." She slid inside the car and leaned over to inspect her lipstick in the rearview mirror.

Bo walked slowly around the back of the car, taking her in. She was perfection. Strong, smart, confident. CEO of her own business. And gorgeous on top of it all. Yet he suspected the old Kiara he'd once loved was still in there. Fun-loving, carefree and wanting only the simple things in life.

Like a family.

He frowned and paused before the driver's side door. Could Kiara be a mom to Emily? No. She was more concerned about making a buck than settling down. A real mum was home for her child, protected them. Wouldn't run away from the father when the tough stuff needed to be discussed. And made dresses with little farm animals on them.

Bo winced. Mums came in all shapes, sizes and skill sets. He shouldn't try to pin one over-all expectation on any woman. And he didn't want to. His mother had always done the best she could. And Bo had survived.

What he and Kiara had started? Had to be just a fling. Much as he preferred otherwise. Because the last thing she probably wanted was to start something with a single dad. A baby could not possibly fit into her new lifestyle.

But what still niggled at him was...how had she found out she couldn't have children? Had she taken a test? Without telling him? It was odd that she'd be seeing a doctor about such a thing while they were dating without any mention of it to him. And, knowing at the time, how dead set he'd been against having a family.

When the question graced his tongue, Bo decided to swallow it. For now. Kiara seemed so happy she was virtually floating. He didn't want to bring her down from that mood with memories of something that had devastated her.

He'd wait.

But not forever.

CHAPTER TEN

THE CAR SLOWED and Bo turned from the gravel road onto a pull-off to rest amid a copse of trees. He put the car in Park and glanced at Kiara. His quirky grin spoke much louder than words.

Kiara moved across the shift and onto Bo's lap. His hands glided up over her derriere and squeezed. Blue eyes locked onto hers.

Some kisses were meant to say things. Some were easy, gentle, polite. Many were an agreement between two people that they belonged to one another and enjoyed sharing themselves. But this kiss was fiery. Urgent. Greedy and sloppy. No politeness or permission required. This kiss said, "Let's do this now. Fast."

Bo's hand at her back clutched her tightly, possessively. He would never let her go. Everything was free and blissful and just as it should be.

He muttered her name against her throat. And she hugged up to him, wrapping herself against his torso, burying her face in his soft dark hair as they found a rhythm together.

Bo pulled into the country estate, a wide grin on his face. The property looked promising. Two stories, brick-fronted, not too large and too small. Geometrically trimmed shrubbery out front, and a stable/barn toward the back. The outbuilding to the left looked like a garage. Plenty of centuries-old oaks, maples…and, man, did he love the weeping willows. They were immense, surely over forty feet tall, and just as wide. Their branches curved gracefully, spilling to dangle but inches from the lush green lawn.

But that wasn't what had put the grin on his face since they'd pulled over five kilometers back.

He looked to Kiara, who was gathering her files and purse. Her hair was tousled from the wind, but the curls that spilled over her cheeks gave her a Botticellian sweetness. Yet he knew better. That woman had taken what she'd wanted from him. And given back.

"What's your first thought?" she said with a gush of enthusiasm. "Looks promising, yes?"

"Are you talking about the house?"

"Of course, I am, Bo, what—" She paused and finally met his gaze. "Oh." She teased her tongue out under her top lip. "I never make promises."

And probably best if he did not, either.

"Tell me about this place." Bo's attention was not on the front of the house, but rather on that narrow column of Kiara's neck. Her hair didn't quite reach her shoulders, so those bouncy curls drew attention to that section of soft, fruit-scented skin. Mmm...

"To be honest, I haven't been in this one. It's a new acquisition thanks to one of my agents. But I've got the sell sheet right here. When I saw the photos I thought it might be a nice contrast to the first property. More homey. But still elegant and worthy of my client."

"Your client?" His heart dropped. "So I'm just the client now?"

"Bo, being my client places you above all others. It is an elite position that I take great pains catering to."

"All right then." Heart back in place? Check. "Cater to me, Duck."

With a tap of her glossy fingernail to her lip, she looked up through her lashes and said, "Thought I just did that."

With a carefree laugh, she took the stairs up to the door. "Let's look at the house, Bo."

After browsing through the house, Kiara left Bo to wander in the garage, which had been built to display the owner's vintage racing cars. Bo thought it would make the perfect gym/garage. When he'd started designing the room out loud, she'd known he would buy this place. He kept muttering how Emily would like that room, or the topiary maze behind the house, or the leaf-shaped wading pool attached to the larger pool.

So she left him to build his dreams and wandered back into the house. It was cool and bright thanks to the modern design and white walls. All the furniture was blond wood, with more white brick and steel accents. Opposite of the previous home. About half the space as well. Bo didn't need any more than the four bedrooms. And the kitchen was large and open to the living area, which had excited him. Great for entertaining.

She headed toward the space next to the kitchen, which was sort of a grand hallway-cum-rest-and-reading-area that had been furnished with cozy white furniture and sat in front of the floor-to-ceiling windows that made up the entire wall. The view was incredible. And she'd left open the doors set into the windows to allow in the scent of wildflowers blooming in the garden.

This was the kind of moment she lived for. That feeling of success. Of having matched a client to a home. And knowing their future would be brighter because of her. All the money in the world could not compete with such a feeling. It was why she would never stop doing what she did.

Stopping before the windows and closing her eyes, Kiara muttered, "I could live here."

The place was perfect. For a family that dreamed of peace and privacy, yet was close enough to a small town for quick grocery runs, and less than a two-hour drive to the Paris apartment if either of the parents had to fly often for work. Or if they wanted to attend the opera or a visit a museum.

She had been lucky these past few years to experience the fine things that money could buy. Thanks to a lot of hard work, she had earned those experiences. The private dinner parties at four-star restaurants, the jet-set lifestyle. Elite hotel rooms, and champagne and caviar. Designer clothing and parties that catered to celebrities.

Yet in the past few days Bo had shown her a new side to life. While she believed everything had to be picture-perfect and controlled, he had shown her things could be a little messy and still work.

If she dropped some of the control and allowed things to just…happen, could she grasp some of the happiness she craved?

With a wistful sigh, Kiara dropped her shoulders. What was she thinking? She was living the dream. Of course, she was happy!

Yet to think on that dream, and the definition she'd created for happiness, made her mouth drop. Another sigh released some of the anxiety she hadn't been aware of.

"Not the dream I signed on for," she whispered. Catching her palm against her chest, she closed her eyes.

In the weeks following the miscarriage and the doctor's diagnosis she had sorted through what her life should have been and what she expected it would become. The idea of adoption had been considered. It hadn't felt right to her. She couldn't even put words to why that was. It just wasn't for her. And there was the surrogate route. Another option that hadn't felt right. Kiara had dreamed of being pregnant. Of wrapping her hands over her swollen belly. Of having two or three children. Of wearing the apron and baking. Building sandcastles with Daddy buried to the toes nearby. And always those dreams had been splashed with her children's laughter.

"What dream was that?"

She tensed at Bo's voice, so lost in her thoughts she hadn't heard him wander in. "Dream?"

"I heard you say this wasn't the dream you'd signed on for."

"Oh. Uh, well…"

Why not confess? He knew what her dreams had once been. It would go some way in making up to him for her withholding all her truths. That one truth that felt too terrible to speak.

"The simple life," she said. It was impossible to speak the next part: *with family.*

"I remember that about you. Something about picket fences. You know, Kiara, you can have a simple life if you want it." He stopped beside her and looked out at the flowers fluttering in the breeze. "I thought you liked this fast and luxurious lifestyle of yours?"

"It's fine. More than fine. I earned it." She surprised herself that she actually had to muster enthusiasm for the announcement.

"Earning something is different from enjoying something. And if you've earned so much, why are you still living in a shoebox?"

"A what?"

He shrugged. "You have the cash, the esteem, the connections, the clothes. Yet you live in a shoebox of an apartment."

"That shoebox is prime real estate!"

"I know. But you need, and deserve, something bigger and better, Kiara. You deserve…a refrigerator box."

She laughed. Bo always made her comfortable with his goofy outlook. "A fridge box?"

"You know what I mean. Something bigger. More fitting of your lifestyle."

"Bigger is not always better. Certainly not simpler when you consider upkeep."

"I know. But do *you* know?"

"Of course, I do." She just had to drop some of the control. It could happen. If she felt confident enough to do so. Possibly even…protected.

He clasped her hand and they stepped to the threshold, where the breeze cooled their faces. Bo inhaled deeply and exhaled. "You like this place, yes?"

"Sure, I love it. It'll be a perfect home for you and Emily. I'd buy it myself if I had the cash to invest."

"Then buy it."

Kiara laughed. "Oh, Bo, that's not how my job works. I'm helping you find *your* dream home. Don't you like this place?"

"Like it? It already feels like home. I want to make an offer on it."

"You do? Yes!" She held up a hand and he met her in a high five. "What do you want to offer?"

"Whatever the asking price is? Go five percent below."

She did some mental math and nodded. "It might work. This is a new listing, though. If they don't like your offer, there's plenty more out there who will snatch it up."

"You're my Realtor, oh, Queen of Luxury Real Estate, so make it happen. For me and my girl."

She almost said, "I'm not your girl." But then remembered he wasn't talking about her.

"Yes, Emily," she said quietly. "And you're close to your mom here. It's a half-hour drive to Caen."

"You did good, Duck." His smile made her heart ache.

"Champagne?"

"Good call." He tugged her to him and kissed her. "Feels right here. But it also feels right standing here with you."

It did feel natural. But stating it did not. Not when she still hadn't been completely honest with him. And the fact that she was thinking about this right now was not a good sign. She couldn't hide it much longer. The truth would hurt him again. She had to stop doing that to Bo. But the tighter she held on to the rest of her secret, the more it cut into her heart.

She had to tell him while she had him alone. But not here. No security cameras to record her personal transgressions for others to watch.

Kiara turned and collected her files and laptop. "It's almost six. The owners will be returning soon. We should get on the road. I'll walk through and make sure everything is locked up."

She exited the room as quickly as she could. Because had she stood in Bo's arms any longer, she never would have left.

Just before she stepped outside to meet Bo at the car, Kiara's phone buzzed.

"Mom," she answered. "Sorry I missed your call. I tried to call a couple times but—"

"Kiara."

The abrupt tone wasn't new, but the breathy gasp following it was. "Mom? What's up?"

"I'll get right to the point, Kiara. I'm…sick."

"What?" Panic fluttered from Kiara's heart and up to her throat. She clasped her neck. "What is it?"

"Now don't freak out. It's not cancer or anything terminal. I don't think. But I will have to undergo a major life change. My adrenal glands are shot. My body isn't keen on fighting infections lately. I just left the hospital this morning."

"Mom! You were in the hospital? Why didn't

you call sooner? Where are you? I'll come right away."

"Not necessary. Listen, Kiara. It was a minor surgery. I'm good right now. Your dad flew in to Berlin, which is where I am right now. He's staying at the hotel with me."

"Give me the address. I can be there by nightfall."

"I don't want you to do that. Dad is with me and they only allow one visitor at a time, anyway. We plan to stop in Paris in a few days. So you just sit tight and wait for us. But I wanted to give you a heads-up on this...thing. It's stress-related. Apparently, the best medicine is to slow down." Her mom's laugh was dry and weak. "You know that will never happen."

"Mom, you need to listen to the doctors."

"I know, I know. We'll talk more about this in a few days. I'd ask to stay with you, but I recall that place of yours is small."

"There's a hotel across the street. I'll make reservations for you and Dad. Please call as soon as you land. I'll send a car for you."

"Don't worry, we'll take care of that. We'll see you soon. 'Bye, daughter."

The connection ended. Kiara stared at her phone. Always, her mother signed off by saying that. Never a more emotional "love you." That wasn't Katherine Kirk's style. Her unspoken title had always been Queen of Emotional Distance.

Her mother had been in the hospital? Due to stress?

Kiara swore.

CHAPTER ELEVEN

DURING THE RIDE back to Paris, Kiara told Bo about her mom's health. She'd had surgery without telling her? Kiara could only imagine it had been an emergency. Bo held her hand during the entire ride. And she loved him for that. They didn't speak much. Sorting her thoughts about what her mother had just laid on her required that she sit quietly with eyes closed. She didn't open them until they entered the city and the neon lights distracted her.

The Lamborghini slowly cruised the narrow Parisian streets. Soon enough, the Ferris wheel flashed into view and wandering tourists who never seemed to obey the traffic signs slowed their journey even more.

"The next block, right?" Bo asked.

"Yes, you know this city well."

He shrugged. "I did live here for three months when I had the dating-show gig."

"I didn't see that one. What did that involve?

Getting naked at a restaurant? Going on random blind dates?"

"The naked-restaurant one was a trip." He kissed the back of her hand and when he made a turn, Kiara pulled out of his grasp. He needed to concentrate on handling the vehicle. "No, the Paris gig was picking out strangers at tourist spots and taking them for dinner. I was supposed to fall in love and propose to one of the half-dozen women." He flashed her a roll of his eyes. "Would have gotten paid double."

"No go?" she wondered.

"Seriously? The Heartbreaker settling down with some random stranger? It was for the camera crews, Kiara. Trust me. I didn't feel a thing for any of them. And when you're being filmed kissing someone? That is the weirdest thing. I walked away from that experience with a new love for Paris, though. Even the tourist spots. You know you can see the entire city from the top of the Eiffel Tower?"

"I do know that. But I can't stand the crowded elevator rides to the top. I prefer the less visited places myself."

"I'd love to see Paris through your eyes."

Kiara swallowed. His voice had softened as they sat at a stop sign, as had his gaze. The sex had been great. It hadn't touched romance or any of the squishy feely emotional stuff that tended to make for relationship material. Which is why she felt so uncomfortable now. Because this was a moment she craved from Bo. And wandering Paris, hand in hand, seeking the secret sites that were uncrowded and peaceful? Yes, please!

And yet… Her emotions had been bouncing all over the place since she'd talked to her mother.

"Someday I'll show you around," she said lightly. "You know me. I don't have the time for a leisurely stroll through any city."

"I do know you." He turned the car down her street. "And what I can tell you? The real Kiara popped out for a while today. When we were parked in the grotto. And a few times in the second house, when you forgot to hold yourself so straight and you laughed along with me. And then again when you told me about your mum. She's going to be okay, Duck. I can feel it."

She lifted her chin at his assessment of her. He was spot-on. Even after she'd hurt him by running away from what could have been something, he was still willing to give her a chance. But she didn't deserve that chance. Not until she was completely honest with him.

He pulled the car before her building and put it in Park.

Kiara let go of the door handle. It was now

or never. And with the parking as it was, he couldn't idle long, so that would allow her a quick escape. The way she preferred things. She'd not yet learned to stand up and face responsibility for the things that gave her the most emotional dread. It was easier to run.

But she did owe him the truth.

"What's up, Duck? You want to talk about your mum some more?"

"No, I can't worry about that until I've seen her and got all the details. Like you said, she's going to be fine. I can feel that, too. I've just a lot on my mind with the sale of the chalet."

"The hard part is over. I want to buy the house. What's got your pretty mouth all frowny?"

"Bo, there's something I need you to know. And I have to tell you quick, then walk away, because it's the only way I know how to do things."

"Walk away?" He turned on the seat, propping an elbow on the backrest. "Kiara, don't do this to me again."

"Huh? No. Again?"

"You planning on walking out on me after this house sale? Seriously, Kiara? I thought we were doing well? Getting to know one another again."

"No, it's not like that at all. I…care about you, Bo. I want us to…be together." Really? Yes! But she should not have let that slip out. "I think it could work."

"I think it can, too. So what's the problem?"

"I wasn't completely honest with you regarding my medical condition. Well, I was. It's as I've explained. I can never carry a child to term. I just left out a detail that I feel, if I'm going to be completely honest, you should know about."

"This sounds serious. Is it something like what your mum has?"

"Oh, no. I don't even know what that— Totally unrelated."

But as far as being stressed out and never taking a break from work? Hell, Kiara knew she was exactly like her mother. And if she was like her mother did that mean she could never truly love a child? Love had been shown with material things when Kiara had been growing up. She couldn't recall when her mother had last hugged her.

"It's all in the past," she said. "Oh, maybe I should just leave it buried where I put it. It's not important now—"

Bo touched her wrist. "What is it, Kiara?"

"I—I didn't just find out about my inability to carry a child out of the blue."

"Oh." He nodded. "Mum wondered about that."

"Your mom?" Her heart thundered now.

"She said there had to be a reason you knew such a thing. Were you seeing a doctor while we were dating? Without telling me? Was something wrong?"

"You think I was plotting behind your back to have a baby?"

"No. I didn't say that. I just think that if this is something you were having a doctor check, I can't believe you didn't tell me about it."

"I didn't tell you about it because I didn't know."

"Then...explain, please. I'll let you talk."

Why had she decided to do this now? Sitting in a convertible that was exposed to anyone who should walk by. There were no people on the street at the moment. Yet, still, the lack of privacy should have detoured her confession.

"Kiara?" Sensing her unease, he looked over the back of the car. "Do you want to go inside?"

"No, I will say this now. Bo, that day that you left for New York for the big fight, I..."

She exhaled, feeling her lungs empty, and along with it hope left as well. She was transported back to that moment when she'd been sitting in the doctor's office, a hospital gown barely covering her shoulders and her legs dangling over the edge. Alone.

Bo leaned over the shift, catching her gaze.

When a tear spilled down her cheek, he touched it, wiping it away. "Tell me, Duck."

If he had been there, holding her hand, would her life have gone differently? Would she have stayed with him? Might they have married? Forged a life without the children she'd so desperately wanted? She would never know. Because she had made a decision out of fear and desperation. Out of a need to take control.

"That afternoon I got terrible cramps, like nothing I'd ever experienced before and... I miscarried. I went to the emergency room and they confirmed it."

"Miscarried? But...you were pregnant?" He thought about it a moment. She watched his expression change to confusion. "How does that work if..."

She nodded. "I didn't know. I swear to you, I didn't know. Sometimes I miss periods, and sometimes I can go two months between bleeding. My cycle has always been erratic that way. I never would have kept my pregnancy a secret from you, Bo. You have to believe that."

"Okay. I believe you," he said softly. "So you only learned about it when...it happened?"

She nodded.

"But you said you couldn't get pregnant..."

"I didn't say that. The doctor ran some tests and the next day she called me back to her office and told me what she found. I would never be able to carry a baby to term. Without getting into the medical terminology, my uterus isn't shaped right and I have only one fallopian tube. I can get pregnant, with great difficulty, but it will never stick."

She inhaled a huge breath and let it sift through her body. Her heart thundered in her ears. She knew Bo was processing. That she should allow him to ask her all the questions. But it was too hard to remain sitting there, in silence. Unknowing if this was the thing that ruined it all. Ended them before they secured a good chance at beginning again.

"That's everything," she said. "I was pregnant without knowing it. I miscarried. I can't have children. I know I just laid a lot on you, but I needed to do it this way. I have to go inside now because the memory of it is simmering inside me. I need to turn on the shower and scream, and then cry. Okay?"

She couldn't look at him. Her lip wobbled. Tears streamed down her cheeks.

Bo leaned over and pulled her into a hug. "Okay. But I wish you'd let me stay with you."

She shook her head frantically. The hug felt... too perfect. And not something she felt she deserved, so she pushed out of it. "Just need to be alone."

"Call me later. Promise."

"I will. You go back to your—" Kiara shook her head, fighting the tears "—little girl."

With that, she released the door latch and slid from the car, taking her things with her. She rushed toward the entry and by the time she began to punch in the digital code, the rental car pulled away.

Kiara turned to face the street. Bo had driven away.

She caught her hand against her mouth. Tears spilled frantically. She shouldn't have told him like that. Should she have asked him inside? Of course. The man had wanted to stay with her. But she'd been too afraid of her own emotions to let him see her so weak. So vulnerable.

Yet now that he was gone, she needed him back.

She'd messed up.

And she'd probably lost him for good.

CHAPTER TWELVE

BEFORE PICKING UP his daughter, Bo exchanged the Lamborghini for a more sensible car at the rental place. Emily was sleepy when he arrived at his mum's house.

Madeline James put a finger to her lips as he entered the dimly lit kitchen. "She's all packed and ready to go. You can probably get her out to the car without waking her."

Bo leaned in and kissed his mom's head. "Thanks, Mum. You've always been good to me. I..."

His sigh pulled out the angst that had been haunting him since Kiara's confession in the car. She'd kept that secret for six years. Just as he and his mum had kept things quiet for much longer. Those unspoken words. The truths he wanted to be out there and in the open.

"I have to say something about Dad. He made our lives tough."

His mom looked up, her eyes watering with tears. She nodded, touched her throat nervously.

"We've never spoken about...how things were," he said carefully, "and I don't want to raise any ghosts for you, but I want you to know that I think we both did our best."

"Oh, Bowen." She gripped his hand and bowed her head, shaking it. "If I could have changed things..."

"I don't think you could have. He was too strong, Mum."

"I'm sorry. I should have taken you away from that man, but... I didn't have anywhere to go. Your father kept the money. I didn't have any close relatives."

"I get it, Mum. I really do."

"But Bowen, you need to know..." She squeezed his hand and pressed it to her cheek.

Bo swallowed. Seeing his mother with tears in her eyes zapped him right back to his childhood. His limbs grew rubbery and he wanted to scream and punch and push away all the bad things that threatened to harm him and his mom.

Finally, she said on a gasp, "You saved me. I only survived with your help. Because, when he started going after you..."

He pulled her into a hug, not wanting her

to have to speak the next part, and not wanting to relive it, either. It was in the past now. But to hear his mum take some responsibility for keeping him in that situation meant something to him.

"You are a good man," she said.

Bo hugged her tighter. Tears loosened in his eyes.

"You are not like him. Don't ever think that you are."

"I'm a fighter, Mum."

"But not like him. Never like him. You'll raise Emily right and love her and protect her."

"I will." And for the first time, he knew, in his heart, that he could. "Thanks for telling me that, Mum. I needed to hear that."

She brushed a tear from his cheek and nodded. With a gesture toward the now-sleeping infant, she stepped back and watched Bo gather her up. He kissed his mum once more then headed back to the airport. Once seated on the plane, he took a deep breath. As simple as the exchange had been between them, it had been necessary. This fatherhood thing? Maybe he could rock it.

Once in the air, Emily woke and began to cry, until the flight attendant managed to produce a perfectly warmed bottle for her. And

Bo's thoughts switched to what Kiara had confessed to him. And that she had pushed out of his hug. Damn, she was really hurting.

She'd been carrying his child? Hadn't known she was pregnant until the actual miscarriage. And yet, when confessing to him the other day about her medical condition, she hadn't felt it necessary to tell him that part. What hell had Kiara gone through? How had she come to the conclusion that *not* confiding in him was best? Had she been afraid of what his reaction might have been? He wouldn't have been cruel to her. He'd never revealed to Kiara how his father had abused him so she couldn't have thought he would— *Had* she thought he'd get violent with her?

At the time, such news would have shocked him, but…hell. What was wrong with *him*?

Could his mum be wrong? Surely, parts of Killian James ran through his veins.

Once at home, Bo tucked in Emily, but didn't read the little board book about elephants that generally put her to sleep. She drifted to the Land of Nod even as he tiptoed out of her room.

He showered, then crash-landed on the bed, arms spread. Staring up in the darkness, the moonlight cast a wide beam across the vaulted ceiling. If he didn't think about Kiara rejecting him—on all levels—then it couldn't hurt him. Just like when he'd avoided his father. If he never got too close, the old man couldn't land a punch.

You're just like me, boy.

He was not his father.

Yes, he hit people. But he did it for a paycheck. And it wasn't a vindictive thing born of a need for violence or to purposely harm another person. He shook hands before and after his fights. It was never personal. But over the years it had served as a means to beat away the memories. And to finally rise above that obsessive desire to hit back at his father. He'd thrown his last "first punch" for his father a few years ago during a fight at Kensington.

Was retirement so easy because he'd finally gotten all his Dad punches out of his system?

Maybe.

He could never find love for that man. At one time in the days immediately following Emily coming to his home he'd thought he needed to forgive to move forward. But that would never happen. His dad wasn't owed that forgiveness.

Bo swore and punched the air a few times, hissing through the movements.

Kiara hadn't trusted him enough to tell him

she had miscarried his child. And Jennifer had not told him she was carrying his child, either.

He jumped up from the bed. Punched the air. Shadowboxing tended to satisfy his craving for exertion, but this was more than that. Anger flowed through his muscles. He turned and delivered a fierce uppercut to an invisible opponent. Bouncing forward, he swung, slipped to the left, and then pulled to a stop before his knuckles could hit the wall attached to Emily's room.

This was not the way to handle things.

Instead he bowed his head and pressed his palms together. His yoga practice did teach him calm. And he needed it right now. Emily must never experience her dad's anger. Ever.

The offer for the property was complete. It just needed Bo's signature. And a two-million-euro check for earnest money. As well, the schedule for viewing his chalet had been set. One of her agents, Rochelle, had already lined up clients to view it in two days. That meant Kiara would have to send in a cleaning-and-staging crew as quickly as possible. It was all rush-rush, and normally she gave her clients more time, but if Bo's offer for the French chateau went through—and it would—she wanted to sell the chalet so he could use that sale to pay on the new property.

A phone call had been out of the question. Especially for her clientele. But returning to the chalet today had been a challenge. Kiara had left Bo after revealing some shocking information. She had no idea what he thought of her. He'd driven away. Without looking back. But worse? He'd had to pick up his daughter after hearing that shocking news.

Kiara had risen above the pain of learning she could not have the one thing she had always desired. Yet there were days when she'd realized that she had been pregnant for six weeks. Pregnant! And if she had known then that she was, she would have reveled in the experience of carrying new life in her belly.

It had been snatched from her so cruelly.

After a tearful shower last night, Kiara had then paced her apartment. Worrying about what she had lost. Worrying about her mom. She'd texted her dad. He'd said it wasn't something she needed to worry about. They'd see her in a few days.

That hadn't reassured her. Nothing brought down the indomitable Katherine Kirk. Nothing.

Hand shaking, Kiara stroked her fingers through her hair as she sat in the rental car in front of the chalet. That she was nervous disturbed her. Yes, her life was stress-filled. Just like her mom's! Would the same thing happen to her? Would stress bring her down and leave her, not only single and childless, but also unable to work at a job that had become her everything?

What she'd begun with Bo—again—felt… right. If anything happened to ruin that, she wouldn't know what to do with herself. She wanted him in her life. But there was no way of knowing how he'd taken her confession last night. Because she'd controlled the situation by leaving before he could fully react.

"Time to let go of some of the control," she muttered. And she meant it.

But meaning something and actually doing it were two different things.

With the forms in hand, Kiara got out of the car and tugged down her skirt. Simple sky-blue today. Not too tight, not too short. Businesslike, but with a touch of softness. The air was steamy, tinged with a sharp pine scent. Cicadas buzzed nearby. It was afternoon. The staging crew would work through the evening. It wouldn't take them long. Just some furniture rearranging and a polish with some window cleaner and mopping would do the trick. Of course, the baby's room would require a quick decorating job.

Walking toward the entrance, relieved there was no media horde clambering in her face, Kiara paused when she heard a noise coming from behind the security wall. A familiar sound. Boxing gloves hitting the heavy bag.

She veered toward the gate and found it was not locked. Peering inside, she spied Bo on the other side of the basketball court, going at the heavy bag suspended from an iron frame by chains. Furiously.

Swinging punches. Landing kicks and elbow jabs. It always amazed her, his agility and ability to swing a punch in one second and land his foot against the opponent's head in the next second. All while keeping up his guard and avoiding the same punishment.

Kiara lingered inside the gate, but the longer she watched, the more it disturbed her. Bo was not in a mere fight with the heavy bag. The chains rattled, the bag bounced, and with each swing of the bag back toward Bo, he pounded it with fists, legs, knees, elbows. Over and over. Sweat saturated him. His gasps were angry growls.

Kiara shivered. What was up with him? He didn't fight like that. The man was actually quite playful, even in a match. It was his style. It had freaked out his opponents on many occasions. She'd never seen him so violent. And she had seen him with blood running down his face and bruises marring every inch of his body.

"Bo!"

One forceful overhand hook sent the bag off the chain. The heavy leather bag landed on the rubber pads with a thud and a spume of dust. Not missing a beat, Bo leaped onto it as if it was an opponent lying on the floor. He punched the bag, kneed it and pummeled it. "Ground and pound" was the term for such a technique.

Worried now, Kiara approached cautiously. It was never wise to step in the ring, or even an open gym, when the fighter was concentrating on what he did best.

"Bo!"

With a growl, he spun up off the bag, charging her. Kiara stumbled backward, her shoulder hitting another hanging heavy bag. Bo's fist raised, but with a flick of his head to redirect the hair from his face, he suddenly pulled back.

"Kiara, what the bloody hell?"

Pacing in a tight circle, he clenched and unclenched his fists, which were encased by the finger-revealing MMA gloves. A panther on the prowl suddenly diverted from its prey. He was angry. He wanted to strike. He needed another punch.

Clinging to the heavy bag, Kiara did not feel as though he'd hurt her. But he had scared her. She needed a few moments for her heart to drop back down from her throat.

"Not smart, Kiara," he growled. "I was in the zone."

"The zone? You were murdering that bag, Bo. What is wrong with you?"

"I'm just—" he pounded a fist into his palm "—working something out."

"So violently? Bo, this is not you. It's— Something must be wrong. You never go at the bag like that. I know you."

"No, you don't!"

"I…" She swallowed the protest and stepped away from the bag, tugging at her skirt to re-sume calmness. "I do know you. Something isn't right. What is it?"

He circled wide toward her. His gaze was fo-cused, as if on his opponent, and it made her step back. As his circle arced him away from her, he kicked at the fallen bag and swore.

"Bo!"

"Kiara!" He spun to face her, tearing away the gloves from his hands and tossing them aside. "I lost a baby!"

"Oh." She caught a hand at her throat. His anger had been hers so long ago. An anger that she had unleashed on him, just as he had been doing to that heavy bag. "Bo, I'm—"

He winced. Panted. Squeezed his fists before him as he modulated his breathing. Finally, he said, "I know, you're the one who lost the baby. But did you even think about me? Did you consider that it might affect me, too? And I'm just finding out now. Six years later."

His predatory circling resumed. "I have feelings, Kiara." He pounded his chest. "I have a heart! And to know that you were carrying my child and then lost it? I grieve!"

"I'm sorry. I know. I…"

No, she'd not known. Hell, at the time, she'd not given Bo's feelings a thought. It had been all about her. Her loss. She'd not considered how it would affect Bo beyond that he'd said he'd not wanted a family and that he wouldn't care.

But he did care. That was obvious in the anger that exploded from him. It was good that she had finally told him. But she should have done it differently. He deserved more from her. So much more.

"And you know the really nutty part about all this?" His circles slowed to a meandering pace. "Two women! Both carrying my baby. Both of them decided it wasn't necessary to tell me I was going to be a father. Both of you!"

She flinched at his shouting. That was something she'd not given thought to since learning about Emily's mother.

"What's wrong with me?" he asked, his voice faltering. He swore. Punched the air a few times. Stopping his pacing, he bent forward, bowed his head and placed his palms on his knees. He looked up to her, sweat beading his face. "Am I such a terrible person?"

Struck by his utter hopelessness, she opened her mouth to respond, but couldn't find the words. The man was hurt. Broken. And her keeping the truth of her miscarriage from him had been responsible for that pain.

Bo dropped forward, landing his knees and palms on the floor mat. Another oath exploded from him. "I don't know what to think, Kiara. As much as my mum tries to convince me I'm not, I really am my father."

"Oh, no, Bo." She plunged to his side and wrapped her arms around his shoulders. His wet head nudged her neck. "You are not like him. You would never harm another person. You treat people well. You are good."

"I harm people all the time, Kiara!"

"That's fighting, Bo. A sport. You shake hands afterward. You know that's different."

He bowed his head against her belly and

curled up before her, so she held him like a child.

"I'm so sorry," she said. "I should have told you at the time. And it wasn't because—"

"Don't lie to me, Kiara. You told me you thought I didn't want a family. You were thinking I wouldn't care. That I would be glad."

"I didn't think you'd be glad. But…" Maybe a little? At the time she certainly had thought he'd be relieved to learn about her miscarriage. "You told me you didn't want a family. I didn't think it would matter to you. And since the baby was gone…well."

He lifted his sweaty head. Eyes that were capable of charming her silly now made her swallow back a gasp of sadness.

"You didn't wait to hear me out when I returned from New York. I would have changed for you, Kiara. I would have loved our child. I would have. I might have thought I didn't want a family at the time, but I really have changed. I promise you, I have. Can you believe me?"

"I know you have changed. You are a father. You have a daughter. You are doing well, Bo. You really are."

"I'm doing the best I can. It's hard. It's really hard."

She hugged him against her shoulder. Never

would she have stepped back into Bo's life if she could have anticipated hurting him like this. The man had been through so much!

"I'm sad about our baby, Kiara. The baby you lost. The baby *we* lost. I guess…murdering that bag right now was that sadness coming up."

She tugged him close. She had hurt him by not telling him. By running away from the problem. Hiding. Sweeping it away and not acknowledging just how much it did hurt. Because it hurt. And, at the time, if she could have punched a bag and screamed and swore, she sure would have.

Holding him, she never wanted to let go. And she did not for the longest time. Well-honed control seeped away, replaced by compassion. An understanding between the two of them. They ached. They had lost. They…had one another.

"Stay with me?" he asked.

"Of course, I will," she said. "I'm here for you. Is… Emily here?"

"She's taking a nap." He gestured to the nearby baby monitor. "Bloody hell, what a mess I am, eh? Sorry—"

"Don't apologize for being a kind, feeling person, Bo. What came out of you in the fight you just had? It needed to happen."

He nodded. "I'm glad you were here to bring

me down. Why are you— I suppose you brought the offer for me to sign?"

"I did. And the cleaning crew arrives in a few hours."

He swore.

"I'll cancel them. It can be put off for a day."

"Thank you. I need some time. *We* need some time, Kiara." He kissed her shoulder and gazed up at her. "We need to grieve our lost child."

CHAPTER THIRTEEN

THE GRIEVING WOULD have to wait. When Emily's burbling sounded over the baby monitor, Bo lifted his head from Kiara's chest. That tyke always woke up happy. Did other babies cry a lot? Not his daughter. She'd cry over a wet diaper, but that was about it.

Kiara pushed the hair from his forehead and kissed his nose. He'd been lost in a weird rage of self-disgust when he'd been beating the bag. Nothing had been resolved. Because he did feel as though they both needed to do more about this, to talk and share their feelings. When they had a moment to themselves.

"Did I ever tell you that your smile makes the angels sing?" he asked, seeking to lighten the moment.

"Hmm…"

"Yeah, and the wind blows, too. Like those dreamy scenes of beautiful women with their hair blowing and the angels singing. You've got that, Duck."

She kissed his forehead again. "If you say so. But those angels do have a certain tone right now."

Bo glanced to the baby monitor. "I have to go to her. She gives Daddy a few minutes and then it's all about her."

"You do what you have to do." With a hand, he helped her to stand and she tugged down her skirt and fluffed her hair, regaining her composure. He wished it was as easy for him. "I brought the paperwork for you to sign. And you'll need to hand me a big check. Then I'll get out of your hair."

"I don't want you out of my hair, Kiara. I'd like you to stay."

"I could do that," she said slowly. "But I need to call the staging crew and reschedule. I'll just…be out here. You take your time. Feed her. Do whatever you need to do. I'm in no rush."

"I get it." Kiara had not yet held Emily. It was probably a big step for her. One he could understand. It had been a step he'd been pushed into, no warning, just go for it. "But I know you're a runner. Please don't run off on me without telling me you're leaving. Deal?"

"Deal."

He rushed off, grabbing a towel he'd left on

the patio table and wiping his face and neck. Working up a sweat was a good thing, but this time it felt as though he was wiping away toxins. Bad things had come out of him. With hope, for good.

Inside the cool house, he found Emily on her back in the crib. She slept in a onesie, which was the coolest name for a piece of clothing. Onesies and kimono wraps and buntings. Baby couture. It gave him a chuckle.

"How's my Chicken?"

He lifted her and knew from the added weight alone she needed a diaper change.

While he changed her diaper, he told her about his day. "That lady you met the other day is back. She's so pretty. She cut her hair, but I like it that length. It shows off her neck. A neck I like to nibble. Just like your toes. Heh. And she's smart. I think we need to take it slow with her, though. She's had a tough time of things. We all have, eh?

"It's all good, though. I think," he whispered to his daughter as he lifted her. She snuggled against his chest, taking in everything as he wandered to the kitchen. "Sorry, I smell like sweat. Daddy's been working out. You know the drill."

He'd had a tough time of things, too. He'd punched out most of his anger. But, damn, he still wasn't right with the world. And having Kiara here only amplified the feeling that something was off and needed to be resolved. Thing was, he wasn't sure how to resolve it. It felt immense while also feeling like a compartmentalized piece of emotion that needed to be placed correctly. Not obliterated, but rather...acknowledged?

He buckled Emily into the high chair and checked the fridge. "We've still got some of those blended peas you had last night. And some turkey that I know you like. Sounds like a four-star meal."

He sat down before the high chair to feed his daughter.

His daughter. Two words he'd never thought he'd think or say. Ever. The Heartbreaker had finally grown up. Or rather, he'd grown into a man who now knew the meaning of pride. And not a superficial pride he got from holding a gold championship belt over his head as the crowd chanted approval. No, this pride felt innate; he was proud to be a dad. Proud to have earned enough to give his daughter whatever she might need. He'd done that. And there was nothing his old man could say to take that away from him.

"You are my daughter and I love you." He

kissed her pea-smeared nose. "Mmm, those are nummy. Do you love me?"

She squeezed some peas through her chubby fingers and reached for his face.

"Yes, I know you do."

After forty-five minutes of sitting on the patio, taking in the sunshine, Kiara got up to check on Bo, and turned to face him. Holding his daughter.

Chill, Kiara, she coached her suddenly thudding heartbeats. *It's just an infant.*

An adorable, smiling baby who looked right at home nestled in the crook of Bo's arm. A tiny pink bow had been clipped in her thick, dark curly hair, giving her a Cindy Lou Who style.

She smoothed her hands over her dress, then twined her fingers together. "Good morning, Emily." The soft, sweet little baby wore a pink onesie that had the word *Heartbreaker* embroidered around the neckline.

Bo bounced Emily playfully. "Mum did that. Remember she used to sew for Dior? My Chicken is much more of a heartbreaker than I am. So did you get the paperwork ready?"

"Yes, you just need to sign. Did you get the check written?"

"My checkbook is in the office. Let's sit a while." He sat on a lounge chair, leaning back with Emily propped on his abdomen, sitting up. The baby reached out toward the trees and cooed. "She loves to bird-watch."

While daddy and daughter tracked a flying wren, Kiara studied Emily. She had Bo's dark hair and pale eyes, but the rest of her was all soft baby and pink bows.

Bo bounced her and the baby reacted with dulcet giggles. "I love me some Chicken toes." He lifted her above his head so her bare feet dangled. Mouthing her toes, he sent Emily into peals of laughter.

"She has the most adorable laugh." Kiara swallowed a rise of breathlessness.

"Do you want to hold her?" Bo asked.

"Oh…" Did she? Hell yes! And yet… Kiara's flight-or-fight reaction kicked her in the chest. She couldn't fight, so the only other option was… "I really need to get these papers signed."

Bo studied her over the top of Emily's head. He was reading her nervousness, her inability to relax and just take in that this was the man he was now. Man plus baby. A set. For the rest of his life.

"Easier for me to sign them if you're holding her. But I get it," he finally conceded. "You know where the office is. Will you run up and grab my checkbook from the top drawer?"

"I'll be right back."

Up in the office, Kiara walked to the window and looked down to see Bo twirling Emily across the basketball court. He was perfect with her. Perhaps the little kid that still lived inside him enhanced his ability to relate to his daughter, made life a little more fun, even goofy.

Hand pressed to her heart, she stepped back from the window. That life—that sweet family—twirling on the court down there could have been hers.

"Don't think like that. You got the life you wanted. Be happy with it."

More an admonishment than an encouragement. But it was what she had.

You could have more. You want more.

She had dropped some of the control, allowing herself to simply react to Bo and the baby. Could she go so far as to hold Emily and experience some of that joy she thought she'd never have?

She was a strong, smart woman. The idea of holding a baby should not frighten her so much!

Opening the drawer, she spied the leather checkbook and grabbed it, along with a capped pen. She hadn't planned to simply fly in, have Bo sign some papers and scamper off again.

But to spend the night meant also spending time with Emily. And Kiara wasn't sure how she would manage that. It wasn't as if she had to *manage* it. She was an adult. A big girl who didn't need to run from every cute baby she encountered. It was dealing with her heart that would offer the challenge. Torn two ways, she wasn't sure which was the best side to take. One was all about work and being rigid. The other way teased at swing sets and picket fences. That untouchable dream that felt so…tempting right now.

Back down on the patio, she laid the papers on the table with the pink tabbed signature lines all in line. Bo had only to scrawl his name, even as he held Emily on one hip.

"Easy enough," she said as she pushed the checkbook toward him. "Now the hard part."

He started to write the check. "It's not hard spending money on something that I know will benefit my family." He pushed the checkbook toward her and she tore out the check. "Thanks, Kiara. You made this easy. I know Emily will love her new home. Won't you?"

Emily giggled.

"Hey." Bo stood and tossed the pen to the table. "Me and Chicken are going to head out on the trail since we missed the prenap walk."

"Oh, sure." Kiara gathered the papers. "Maybe I'll run inside and make some lemonade for when you get back."

He shrugged. "You do your thing. If you want to join us, you'll find us on the trail."

He grabbed a woven scarf that had been strewn across a chair and began an elaborate wrap about his body that secured Emily to his chest, facing out, legs dangling. He did it like a pro. Like an experienced parent.

With a nod to her, Bo wandered off and immediately started a conversation with Emily.

After sliding the signed documents and check into her briefcase, Kiara snapped it closed. As she wandered into the chalet, she felt a weird resistance when crossing the threshold. Like some force was pushing her back outside.

Kiara closed her eyes, knowing exactly what the sensation meant. She should have held Emily. Just a moment to experience the sweetness in her arms. It might have provided a balm to her sadness. How could baby giggles not cure a broken heart? And then she could hand her back to Bo. No harm done.

"What are you doing, Kiara?" she whispered. "You can't live your life this way." Not when her mother had just gotten out of the hospital for living the same lifestyle. She was… "Throwing away an opportunity."

A moment to hold her dream. To show Bo that she really did care about him. And everything he cared about.

You have to do this. Or you'll regret it later.

Turning abruptly, she marched back outside and joined Bo as he opened the gate that led to the trail.

"I'm in for the walk," Kiara said. "But only if I get to hold the chicken for a little while."

Bo's expression had never been more ebullient. With a nod, he gestured that she should take the lead.

When they paused at the turnaround bench, Bo bounced softly, keeping Emily entertained. That Kiara had come along with them gave him hope. And relief. Yes, she had a terrible medical condition that would deny her from ever becoming the mother she had always dreamed to be, but if she could find some joy in other babies then that was a good thing. Right?

Oh, you crazy bloke. You broke your rule! You let Kiara back into your heart.

And he was perfectly fine with that right now.

"I've been thinking," Kiara said as she paused, hands on hips, to look out over the valley.

"Yeah? More so than usual? Because I don't know how you keep it all straight in that gorgeous brain of yours."

Kiara smirked. "I've been thinking about… slowing down."

Bo did an abrupt turn at that announcement. "Did I just hear Kiara Kirk say she wanted to slow down?"

"Don't make a big thing out of it, you goofball. I'm just… Well, my mom's issue got me to thinking. A lot. I don't want stress to bring me down like it did her. You know?"

"Stress will do that. And if you don't have an outlet for it…"

"Like punching heavy bags?"

He shrugged. "Works for me."

"I might take a stab at one of them."

"Uh, you don't stab the bag, Kiara. It's a punch. Show her, Chicken." Taking Emily's chubby little fist, he made the punching motion, slowly, as if explaining to an idiot.

"Are you being sarcastic?"

"Not me. Emily did it." He winked. "How's it working?"

She shook her head. "I deserved that one. Yes," she said to Emily, "even from you. Anyway, it's just a new thought. Not sure I'll do anything about it. But there it is."

"If you ever want to learn to punch the heavy bag, I'm your man."

"I'll keep that in mind." She bent to check Emily's face. Round blue eyes brightened and her head swiveled at the sound of a bird chirping. "She really does love walks. She's so quiet and observant of everything."

"Taking in the world. She's smart. What's that, Emily? You want the pretty lady to hold you? What do you think, Duck?"

Kiara surprised him with her immediate response. "I'd love to."

Kiara held out her hands and Emily leaned toward her, much as she did when Bo was with his mom. She liked women. Should he take his mom's suggestion and begin a mom hunt for his child? Infuse some feminine energy into his daughter's life? He didn't even need to answer that obvious question.

"You got her?" he asked as Kiara hefted Emily into her arms and adjusted her hold. "What do you think, Chicken? The pretty lady smells nice, eh?"

Emily bounced her legs against Kiara and looked up at her, grasping for the ends of her hair. They walked slowly, Kiara studying Emily and Emily studying her. Coming to terms with one another. Deciding who was in charge.

Kiara had no idea this little girl ruled them all.

With a smirk at his thought, Bo bounced ahead, shadowboxing. It was like breathing. He had to move, to go through the motions that were more normal than walking to him. And this time he wasn't beating an invisible enemy that lived in his past. Vivacious energy filled him with happiness.

"You look good holding her," he said to Kiara. Best to reassure her, right? Cover all possible angles to keep her from fleeing.

"She's so precious. It's almost..."

Kiara stopped walking. He could see her lower lip wobble, her chin tighten. Something deeply emotional was erupting right about—

"Bo."

"I can take her." Too much, too soon, he decided. At the very least, he had tried.

Kiara handed over Emily. Then she started a fast walk toward the house. "Sorry! I just..." She picked up into a jog.

Bo kissed Emily's cheek and hugged her. "It's not you, Chicken. She'll come around." He sighed. "Maybe."

CHAPTER FOURTEEN

AFTER A BOTTLE out on the patio, Emily snoozed against Bo's shoulder. He wandered inside and found Kiara in the kitchen. The pitcher of lemonade had a few mint leaves swirling with the ice cubes.

"You okay?" he asked.

"Yes." She heaved out a sigh and slid a leg onto the barstool to sit. "I'm sorry, Bo. And Emily. It was terrible of me to run off like that."

"No need to apologize. I think I understand."

"Do you?"

"First, you have a lot on your mind after hearing about your mother. Second, it's gotta be tough spending time with me and Emily—"

She put up a palm to stop him and he did.

"Emily is perfect," Kiara finally said. "And she smells great. Just like her daddy."

"Must be something in our genes."

"Must be. You know, I considered adoption for a while."

"Yeah?"

"It didn't feel right for me. I know single mothers can adopt, and there are so many babies in the world that need good homes. And there's also surrogacy. But again, it didn't feel like a fit for me. It's difficult to explain beyond that it's something I know in my gut. If I can't give birth to a child, then I'm not sure I was meant to have one. Maybe it was some higher power's means of saying I'm not fit to love a child. And, you know, the idea of a baby once fit my lifestyle. But not any longer."

Bo slid his hand across the counter to touch her fingertips. "Kiara, I believe you would make an amazing mother. Don't think otherwise. And if God, or whoever or whatever it is you believe in, wouldn't give you a child, that does not mean you still can't be a mother. What I'm trying to say is, don't blame yourself."

"Thanks. I try not to. But it's hard."

"I get that. I had a chat with Mum the other day. For the first time I learned that she thought *I* had saved her from my dad." He rubbed his jaw. "She doesn't think I'm like him, either."

"You're not, Bo. I'm so sorry you had to grow up like that."

"Thank you. But hearing Mum say it changed things for me. Maybe Emily will have an okay daddy after all."

"Bo," she quickly said. "You do the daddy thing well. In fact, it looks like a baby is a perfect fit for you. Surprising as that may have been to you. I admire you for the way you are living your life. You were handed a challenge, and you've risen to it. I'm proud of you."

Such words to hear. It meant something to him. And hearing it from Kiara made his heart explode.

"Did I say something wrong?" she asked.

"Nope, you just made me happy, Duck."

So she was doing this. Accompanying the family James on an errand. It felt out of her norm. Like she was a third wheel? Kiara wasn't sure how to label it. Bo and Emily were tight. And she was the lady walking alongside them. An outsider. Something didn't fit. Until... Bo reached for her hand and clasped it.

Kiara met his gaze. His soft blues smiled warmly. The little chicken snuggled against his chest peered at her. Did Emily's mouth crinkle into a lazy smile?

Okay, so maybe this something did feel a tiny bit right. In a weird way. It was almost as if she was playacting at the one thing she'd wanted for so long...but knew it could never be hers, so she'd just take what she could of it.

That felt greedy and not at all like her. But she

wanted to do better. And next time Bo offered to let her hold Emily, she would not run away. Seriously. She'd overcome that hurdle.

As they approached the pub, she didn't let go of Bo's hand. A squat two-story establishment fronted with massive fieldstones, it advertised local brews and *saucisson vaudois* in bright white letters scribbled on the front window. Karaoke was every Wednesday night.

Kiara whispered a silent blessing that it was Monday.

Bo tilted his head toward hers to whisper, "Paparazzi at eight o'clock. Don't look. Keep walking." He picked up their pace and hustled them inside the pub. "Just when you think they've all crawled back into their holes, a straggler crawls out sniffing for crumbs."

Kiara walked carefully around the giant ostrich carved out of a tree trunk situated smack-dab in the middle of the entrance. "I don't know how you can spot them like that."

"A dude in dark sunglasses with a monster camera hanging around his neck? Shouldn't you have mastered the spot with all the celebrity clientele you work with?" He nodded to the bartender and directed Kiara toward a corner table by the window.

Kiara slid onto the hard wood bench, thanking the bartender for the water he brought to the table. "I've experienced minor celebrity with the Queen of Luxury Real Estate label, but much as Lyle wishes otherwise, nobody is taking pictures of me. Not unless it's at one of my clients' parties."

"The guy outside just got one of both of us."

Kiara's shoulders dropped. "Oh."

"Emily was probably in the pic, too," Bo said. "I hope her face was covered. The last thing I want is my child's image out there. They can't legally do that. I will sue them if it ever happens."

"She's very lucky to have a smart dad like you."

"I'll take smart." He sipped his water. "But my first reaction is always to punch instead of sue."

"Just be careful those punches don't land you in trouble because you were trying to protect your family. Emily needs her daddy out of jail."

"I am careful. But that's another reason I want to move. This feels like a new beginning. Sure, the paparazzi will find me in France, but eventually they won't care about the retired fighter. I mean, why do they even care in the first place?"

"It's your personality. You're fun to watch. You're sexy as hell. And you give good show. The camera loves you. Or so I've been told. I didn't catch all of your television appearances."

"Screw those stupid TV shows." He loosened his shoulders and turned on the charm. "You think I'm sexy?"

"You know I do, Casanova."

"I like that name better than Heartbreaker. Emily can have that one."

"I thought she was Chicken?"

"She is *my* Chicken. No one else can claim her that way." He kissed the infant's head and she yawned and opened her eyes.

The bartender appeared with two plates and a smaller plate with something orange on it. "Smashed summer squash," the burly man announced proudly. "The wife figures your little 'un will love it."

"Thanks, Sven." Bo fist-bumped the man.

"I didn't even order," Kiara said as she looked over the huge serving of sausages, potatoes, gravy and what might be brown-sugared squash.

"There's only one meal a day here. You don't like it? Don't come back."

"I like it."

And she wasn't talking about the food.

They made an evening of dinner, even chased a flock of geese in the field out behind the pub, and afterward picked up some groceries. Back at Bo's place, the sun settled behind the forest horizon. Emily had begun crying five minutes earlier. He strolled inside, grabbed a bottle and headed up to the nursery, calling back for Kiara to make herself at home.

She intended to. And she wouldn't argue that she should spend the night anywhere else. Why not sleep with Bo? They'd had sex a few times already. And she wasn't stupid.

But what was she, exactly?

She wasn't his girlfriend. He was her lover. For the moment. She was quite adept at the one- or two-night hookups. Preferred them, actually. Made life simpler. She hated complicated. Save that for contracts and the big sell. That was where she shone. When she had sex, she wanted it to be easy, satisfying, but not something that required she care.

Plopping onto the couch and kicking off her shoes, she tugged out her phone to check what Lyle had posted to their socials. There was a problem with her carefully constructed life rules. She did care. About Bo. About the fact that they really did work well together. About the gorgeous new home he was going to move into all by himself.

With Emily.

The one thing that made her tippy-toe around the issue of getting back together with the only man who had ever intrigued, indulged and satisfied her was an innocent little baby. Sure, she had dropped her guard and had begun to feel more comfortable around the little tyke. But it didn't feel right to step in and claim a position as caretaker for her. Not that she would ever label herself Emily's mom. But to share Bo's life included Emily.

Kiara had expected some emotions during this sale for Bo. But not so many and them being so constant. The man didn't realize how sexy he looked with Emily wrapped against his chest, her little head nestled below his chin as he walked. Every so often Bo leaned his head to give her a kiss. And that Kiara thought it was sexy surprised her. Give her muscles, a sexy smirk and a charming demeanor, and she was sold. But dad vibes had never done it for her.

"This can't be good," she muttered as she scrolled through her emails.

Nothing from Lyle. Lucy had emailed her about the Caen property, wondering if the offer was firm. She had a client interested in it. Kiara texted back to take it off the market; Bo had already handed over earnest money.

And if for some reason he backed out on the buy? She may snatch up that place for herself. The news from her mother had set her off-balance. Perhaps it was time she treated herself. Or rather, allowed herself to take a step into relaxing, to creating a real life for herself. A life that included her work, but also allowed her to explore the woman she had once been. Bo seemed to think she was still in there. And he did have a manner of teasing her out.

Opening Instagram, she scrolled randomly while she waited for Bo. Lyle had posted images of Rochelle's recent sale. A sweet penthouse in Mitte, the central district of Berlin, that featured high ceilings, all-steel furnishings and a walk-in wine closet that could hold over twenty thousand bottles. Selling price: a cool eight million. Rochelle liked to work in Berlin, it being where she grew up. And Kiara was fine with that. She knew the city well and Rochelle's former profession as a hip-hop singer allowed her to connect with the young and trendy set.

Scrolling away from the Kirk Prestige Homes, Kiara mindlessly took in the stream. She followed luxury realty sites, some beauty influencers and a lot of silly cat accounts.

When she scrolled past a pair of familiar faces, her heart suddenly pounded. Kiara slashed upward and studied the photo of her and Bo walking hand in hand outside the village pub. Emily was wrapped against Bo's chest, her face not visible. Thank goodness. They'd caught Bo looking at Kiara with admiration. And she was looking at him with…lovestruck adoration.

When she read the caption, Kiara's heart caught in her throat.

Has the Heartbreaker found a mother for his child? Is the Queen of Luxury Real Estate ready to turn in her designer handbag for a diaper bag?

She swore, not too quietly. How dare the reporter make such an assumption? It had literally been less than four hours since the photo had been taken.

She read the byline. It was attributed to an international news rag that thrived on celebrity and political scandals.

"Found a mother for his..." She sat upright. Saying it, and considering the ramifications at the same time, altered something in her.

Was *that* the reason Bo was being so nice to her? He was seducing her. Trying to impress her with his changed ways?

"No," she whispered. Sure, Emily did need a mother. But Bo had given no indication he was mom-shopping for her.

"Emily's asleep." Bo came flying over the back of the couch, landing on a cushion beside her.

His landing wobbled Kiara so she adjusted

her position, stood and stepped toward the window. "Bo, what are we doing?"

The man's jaw dropped. He made a show of looking around. "I've sensed a change of tone in the room. What did I miss?"

"I'm just wondering—well, what are we doing. Together? With Emily? Did you see this?" She turned her phone screen toward him.

He leaned toward her and grabbed the phone. "Bastards! That didn't take them long. Emily's face is covered. Lucky for them."

"Read the text."

He did, then shrugged. "Queen of Luxury Real Estate. That's who you are."

She avoided his attempt to grasp her hand and instead walked around the sofa and toward the front door.

"Seriously?" He followed her. "Are you going to run away from what feels like another fight? Is that your thing now, Kiara? Am I going to have to deal with this every time we—"

"Every time we what?" she snapped at him. "You think I'm sticking around when all you care about is finding a mother for Emily? I can't believe I was such a sucker for your sweet-daddy act."

She grabbed the door handle, but Bo slammed his body against the door. She would have to shove him aside to open it. Or deliver a smart kick to his thigh. Instead, she stepped back, hands on her hips. She realized now her shoes were still sitting by the couch. And where she intended to run to, she didn't know.

"I'm not looking for a mom for Emily," he insisted in a firm but quiet voice. He glanced up the stairs. No baby cries. Yet. "You have a tendency to make assumptions about me, Kiara. And they are generally wrong."

"I wasn't wrong about leaving you six years ago. You wouldn't have known how to help me then."

He gripped her by the shoulders, a soft fury growing in his eyes. But just when she thought the fighter would step out and shove her aside in favor of finding some inanimate object to punch, he breathed in through his nose. Eyes closing, his fingers loosened their grip but did not let her go. With an exhale, he opened his eyes.

"You're right," he said calmly. "I wouldn't have known what to do then. But I would have tried my damnedest to do whatever you asked of me. Did I ever deny you anything?"

Well, now he was just being sincere. Tears heated the corners of her eyes. Why couldn't he just let her run away? Life was so much easier when she didn't have to stand up and face it. This letting-go-of-control thing was so difficult!

"Maybe we weren't meant to be back then," he said. "Maybe we're not meant to be now. Though, I feel differently. I love you, Kiara. I always have."

She shook her head but couldn't find words to deny the love he declared for her. No words to confirm it, either. She loved him as well. But to say such would surrender to...

To what? To letting go of that last bit of control she'd held in a firm grip since turning her life around that night she'd first walked away from him?

Things had changed. Bo had changed. She... was changing. Or maybe, she was beginning to turn around, and look back at the woman she had once been. A woman she could never completely abandon.

"Yes," she whispered. Then, with tears coming, she said it again. "Yes. You would have done your best. And I should have given you that chance. I'm sorry, Bo. But I don't know what this is now. Between us. It feels like... I don't even know. Don't you want a mother for Emily?"

"Of course, I do. When I see her with you, or my mum, I realize she needs a woman in her life. And I know someday I'll find that for her. But seriously? That sounds so wrong. Find a mom for Emily? Like I have to go on a search? It should be more natural. Like it just happens."

"Nothing just happens, Bo."

"Yeah, it does. Look at us. Here we are again. Falling in love. It's like the universe couldn't keep us apart. Don't shake your head. You know it's true. But me and you?" He slid his hand along her neck. The warmth of his fingers softened her need to escape. Redirected her instinct to flee. "I don't look at you and think 'there's Emily's mom.' I think 'there's the woman I love.'"

Kiara let the tears fall without stopping. She leaned against Bo and he kissed her head and wrapped his arms around her. It shouldn't bother her that he'd consider her mom material. It should make her incredibly proud. But the way it had been presented in that Instagram post had ruined it for her. She may never be good with this aspect of her life.

It was not cool that she could not move beyond it.

There's the woman I love...

He loved her. Bo could love her after everything she had done to make it impossible to love her. The man was either an idiot, or his doctor was wrong and he had taken on some brain damage in the ring.

"I just want you to be happy," he said quietly.

"Work makes—"

"That's a lie," he interrupted. "Work fulfills you. It gives you a purpose. But it doesn't make you happy. You just need to remember who you are, Kiara."

When had he become so insightful! "That woman is long gone."

"No, she's standing aside for the moment. And trust me, allowing yourself to love me? That won't get in the way of the working woman who is currently in control. But it might bring back some of the lost girl inside you." He bowed his head against hers and hugged her tightly. Then, with a sigh, he asked, "Do you want to end up like your mom? In the hospital because of stress?"

"No, I don't," she whispered. "And I do miss the Kiara you once knew. The one who dreamed of family."

"Then don't be so hard on her," he said. "Take her out once in a while and let her play."

She smiled against his chest. "I think all the meditation and yoga has done something to you."

"Good, bad, or ugly?"

"Very good."

They stood there, hugging, not needing to say much more. Kiara knew she was wrong about her life. She had fled during a dreadful time, a life-changing moment, and had pulled a one-eighty that would not allow her to incorporate any of her real, genuine self into the new version. But Bo was right. That woman needed some attention.

"I've been thinking," Bo said. "We need to do something. It's important. And it might be a new beginning for both of us."

"I don't understand."

"Will you stay with me here tonight?"

"I…well, sure. But I'm still a little…" Unsettled about this discussion. How to move forward? Where to begin? Would Bo be there holding her hand and helping her along? It felt very fast. But as well, it felt right.

"You go upstairs and take some time to yourself. I know that's your thing." He smudged a tear from her cheek with his knuckle. "Meet me outside in about an hour. I'll have something I want to show you. Do you trust me?"

"I've always trusted you."

"Not necessarily true, but I'll take it. And tiptoe past Emily's room, will you? She's always a little light when she first falls asleep."

She nodded, and Bo left her before she could protest. He dashed through the kitchen and down the hallway toward the patio.

Kiara sighed. What was she doing? The door was right there. She could open it, hop in the rental car and flee before he realized she had made an escape.

No. She owed him more than that. And besides, she did not want to run away this time. He loved her. And it took a strong man to see beyond her flaws, mistrust issues and downright concealing of truths.

Could she follow her heart? That was not what the Queen of Luxury Real Estate did. She never broke her icy veneer.

No, someone else had broken it. And it felt pretty damn good.

CHAPTER FIFTEEN

AFTER A SHOWER, Kiara fluffed out her hair and slipped into the long ruby silk nightgown she'd packed. It wasn't sheer and could pass as a dinner party dress if a person didn't know better. She didn't feel weird about going out to meet Bo wearing it. He'd seen her naked.

Strolling past Emily's room, the door partially open, she peeked inside. A pulsing mood light gave off a minuscule intermittent glow. The room smelled of baby lotion and lavender. The big stuffed bear had been moved by the staging crew to sit on the chair. Emily's crib sat beneath a sprinkle of gold stars.

Bo was one lucky man.

And so was Emily. She had a dad who cared about her. Above all else.

And Bo cared about Kiara. She knew that now. She did trust him. And really hoped they could figure out this relationship they'd stepped back into.

"I should have held you longer," she whispered. "I could have. It was that part of me that is afraid to return to the old Kiara." The one who believed in happily ever after. "Promise next time I'll surrender to all your giggly goodness."

And she would. It felt right in her heart. She wasn't afraid of Emily. It might be a little bit of intimidation. Emily held Bo's heart firmly in her chubby little grasp. Was there room for Kiara as well?

"Sleep well, little one."

In the kitchen, she grabbed a bottle of Bo's branded water and tilted back a few swallows. It had been a crazy day. Exhaustion softened her shoulders. But she also wanted to see what Bo had waiting for her outside.

The lanai doors were open. Pine and a hint of chlorine perfumed the air. She was led forward by the twinkling of dozens of candles placed on the table, the patio floor, the basketball court— and beyond that, more candles flickered. Bo stood before those candles, hands stuck in his pockets, waiting for her.

"What is this?" She padded barefoot across the basketball court. "It's so peaceful."

"Good. I found all these candles in a box when I moved in. Finally have a reason to use them. I was going for a reverent, soulful feel."

"Bowen James, you certainly have changed. I'm pretty sure *reverent* and *soulful* have never been words in your vocabulary. A guy starts doing yoga and suddenly he's a Zen master."

"Far from it, but I'll keep striving. Come here." She took his hand and he pulled her in for a hug. "You smell like my spicy shower gel. And how sexy is that dress?"

"It's a nightgown. I did intend to stay the night."

He kissed her and stroked aside a strand of her hair from her brow. "That means a lot to me."

"So what's up? Why the candles? Are you romancing me?"

Again, he kissed her, but softly. Testing. Or maybe simply taking his time. He moved to nuzzle against her neck, and lingered there. She loved feeling him against her skin. Knowing that he was scenting her, losing himself in her.

"I wish this was about romance, but it's not." He gestured to the scattering of candles. Kiara noticed the thick white center candle was not lit. "I don't want you to get angry with what I'm about to say."

"I won't. Promise." She clutched his hand with both of hers. It did sound ominous, but she owed him acceptance. And she'd grown up in the past few days. Time to pull down those last bits of armor she'd wrapped about her heart. "What is it?"

"I feel like you never grieved for your lost child. I mean, it sounds like you jumped right into work and becoming the boss lady as a means to avoid facing that devastating blow."

He wasn't wrong. "I had to do something, Bo."

"I know."

"And I have mourned the fact I can never have a child."

"But did you mourn the baby you lost?"

"Well, I…"

She hadn't specifically done anything to grieve the loss. Just as she'd missed enjoying the fact she had been, briefly, pregnant. At the time she'd been too caught up in the tragedy of her life. She hadn't separated her anger from the grief over losing a baby, as undeveloped and small as it had been. It had been an overall dread that she'd not compartmentalized into pieces; a means to not completely falling apart.

"And me." He squeezed her hand. "I just learned that I would have been a father six years ago. But that baby wasn't meant to be a part of this world. It affects me, Kiara."

"I know, Bo." She hugged up alongside him and tilted her head onto his shoulder. "I'm sorry, I should have told you."

"You did what you had to do. I don't blame

you for running away. I honestly don't. But we both need to grieve our lost child. And I thought, well…" He splayed his hand toward the candles. "We could do something now. Light a candle for that brief soul."

"That sounds…"

"You can tell me if you think I'm being stupid."

"I think it's a lovely idea. I want to do this." She tilted onto her tiptoes and kissed him. "Thank you."

"It's for both of us. So…let's kneel and give some thought to the little one?"

She nodded. Together they kneeled before the candles. Flames warmed Kiara's skin and glowed across Bo's face. It felt reverent.

Bo set a lighter on the stone surface beside her knee. "Can I say something? For our baby?"

"Yes," she said, her voice wobbling.

The immensity of what was taking place humbled her, made her shiver. But at the same time, she was overwhelmed by Bo's kindness and genuine desire to, in a meaningful way, claim their child. Make it real in a manner she'd never thought to do at the time. Had been too traumatized to even consider.

"Did you name the baby?"

She shook her head. "It was only six weeks.

It was…" She wasn't about to describe that experience to him.

"I get it. So let's call our baby… Star. A little star that went to heaven before we got to meet the tyke. I believe that we all come to this earth with a purpose. I even believe that some souls are destined for one another. Like you and me. And maybe Star's purpose was ultimately to make a brief appearance that would leave a mark on both our lives."

Tears spilled down Kiara's cheeks. He was so beautifully eloquent.

"For whatever reason you came here, we love you, Star." He handed her the lighter.

Kiara took it and paused. Should she say something as well? Bo had covered it. A soul meant to touch their lives.

She let out a sigh mixed with an exhale. And in that moment she felt Bo's strength. His kindness. Indeed, they had been meant for one another. And they had found their ways back to the place they belonged. A place that had been briefly visited by their child. Which meant, she actually had been a mother. For a flicker of time.

And to think of it that way lightened the heaviness in Kiara's heart.

She leaned forward and lit the final candle.

It sparked and flashed, the flame lifting high before settling to a fat golden shimmer.

"That was cool," Bo said. "Sort of like Star. A brief flash."

Tears falling freely now, she nodded and buried her face against his chest. He hugged her close, and they kneeled amid the flickering candlelight, quietly, hands clasped.

CHAPTER SIXTEEN

THE NEXT MORNING, Kiara kissed Bo as they stood in the chalet threshold. Then she leaned in and kissed Emily on the head.

"Oh, soft baby hair!" she said to both of them. "It's such a treat to nuzzle." Emily managed to grab one of Kiara's fingers and she delighted in the moment.

And Bo could have shouted with joy as he felt his heart swell. Finally, Kiara was coming around and allowing herself to get comfortable with Emily.

"Let me give her a hug before I go," Kiara said.

This time, Kiara took the baby with an assurance that made Bo realize she knew what she was doing. The old Kiara, who had once told him that babysitting had been the catalyst to her desire for family, was creeping up to stand alongside the boss lady. Emily melded against her chest, her eyes looking upward, seeking her gaze. Kiara smiled down at her and kissed her nose.

Gently, she hugged her, finding a subtle rocking motion similar to how he rocked Emily. There was a mother within Kiara Kirk. It had never been banished, despite her attempts to do so while climbing the real estate ladder to her throne.

Bo suspected he wouldn't even have to prepare for a quick take-back this time.

"You're so strong," Kiara said to Emily. "Like Daddy!" She kissed the baby's head. "You smell good, too. Unlike Daddy after he's been working out. Right?"

"She doesn't want you to leave," Bo said. "I don't, either."

"Oh, Bo, believe me, I want nothing more than to spend time with you, getting to know Emily. She feels so good in my arms."

"Hold her as long as you like." He leaned against the doorjamb. "My two girls finally getting to know one another. I've never felt happier."

"I feel pretty happy myself. But you know I have to leave. Mom and Dad arrive in Paris this afternoon. I want to meet them at the hotel."

"You want me and Chicken to fly in tomorrow? Be there to support you if needed?"

"That sounds great. But I don't want you dragging Emily all over, hopping planes and catching limos. And really, it's too much to ask that you drop everything for me."

"Eh, Emily likes flying because she's a master at wrapping the flight attendants around her little finger. How soon before me and Chicken can move into our new place?"

"If we rush things through, a month. The family is fine with an early closing. And remember tomorrow there's two viewings of this place."

"Good reason for me and Emily to visit you in Paris."

And to stay in her life. This spending-days-apart scenario? It felt wrong. Now, more than ever, he wanted Emily and Kiara to bond.

"I agree."

Bo wrapped an arm around Kiara's back and leaned in to kiss her slowly, lingering in the heat of their connection. He felt Emily's fingers tickle at his hair, and it couldn't have been a more perfect moment. They had done something amazing together last night by honoring Star. Something had settled into his heart when that flame had burst. And it felt welcome.

Now, to move forward.

"She feels so good," she whispered.

"I think she could fall asleep in your arms," Bo said.

"So that's her sneaky plan, eh?" Reluctantly

she handed Emily back to him, but lingered, smoothing her fingers over Emily's curly hair. "I can't wait to see the two of you again."

"Say hi to your parents for me. And remember to breathe, okay? Your mum is going to be fine."

"Thanks, Bo." She toggled the baby's feet. "See you soon, Emily."

"What do you think, Chicken?" he asked as Kiara strolled out to the rental car. "Are we ready to make an even bigger change than moving?"

Emily let out a long cooing sigh that made him laugh. She was right. And he knew exactly how to facilitate that change.

Kiara had reserved a room for her parents at the Hotel Regina. They texted her upon arriving at the airport and wanted to meet for a late lunch. Kiara told them to bring their things to the hotel first, where she now waited. She didn't want to discuss her mother's medical condition in a public space.

The room was elaborately decorated to look like something out of a Louis XIV-era boudoir. Fresh calla lilies jutted from a porcelain vase. A welcoming tray of sugary pastries and juices had been placed on the dining table. Pacing before the open patio doors, Kiara avoided over-thinking about her mom. She'd learn all the details soon enough.

What did occupy her thoughts was how hard it had been to walk away from Bo and Emily and get in that rental car. She didn't want to be here in Paris. And Lyle's text reminding her she had a viewing with a client in Venice in two days actually annoyed her. Did she have to work so much? She wanted to be wherever Bo and Emily were. To hold that sweet little baby again. But really, could that happen?

Was she ready to allow that to happen? Having a baby, even if she was only Bo's girlfriend, who was allowed to care for Emily, meant giving up control. Babies were messy. They had their own schedules. They did not understand work hours and client meetings and flying across Europe to seal the deal.

"The agency is doing well," she said, giving herself a pep talk as she paced. "If I hire another agent that will free up some of my time. Bo loves me. He loves Emily."

Could *she* love Emily? Dare she even consider she might step in as Emily's mother? Bo hadn't suggested any such thing, even when she'd accused him of doing just that. But again, as a girlfriend, she could be there, share time with Bo in raising his daughter.

"It's been a long time since I've taken care of

a baby." Back to pacing. "And they are a lot of work. I'm gone a lot. Traveling. Flying all over Europe. Emily deserves someone who will be home more often. Oh!"

When had she forgotten that she was determined to never step into the dream of being a mother? Had it been that kiss from Bo? No, it had been just hours earlier, when she'd held Emily against her heart and had known that she could love her.

The door to her room opened and in walked her parents. Kiara rushed to her dad and landed in his generous bear hug.

"You look incredible K-K," he said. He'd called her that since she was a toddler.

"So do you, Dad. I've missed you. It's been almost a year!"

"Miss you back, sweetie." Tall and lanky, her father wore his silver hair shaved short, and a salt-and-pepper moustache. "We need to solve this long-distance relationship we've got going on. And soon."

"I do work in Europe. I'm not sure…" She spied her mom over her dad's shoulder. She'd made her way to the chair by the open patio door. Her long silver hair was pulled up in a messy bun, which wasn't Katherine Kirk's smooth, controlled style at all. And she looked frail.

"Oh, Mom." Kiara kissed her on the cheek and gave her a light hug around the shoulders. Her mother had never been demonstrative with affection. And while she wanted to crush her in a hug, Kiara didn't know how to instigate such closeness between them.

Because an intimate hug meant approval. As she'd learned by holding Emily.

She kneeled beside the chair and smoothed a hand down the leg of her mother's blue linen slacks. The studious daughter taking her place at her mother's feet. "How do you feel? You look…" So pale. "Tired."

"I feel well, Kiara. As much as I enjoy flying all over the world, just getting on a plane throws me, you know that. It's that dry air. Ugh. I need to hydrate and eat and I'll feel much better."

Her dad poured a glass of water from the pitcher and handed it to Katherine.

"Your dad and I are headed to Greece after our stay in Paris to catch some sun."

"Greece? Should you be traveling so much? You just got out of the hospital. Tell me everything. Please?"

They moved out to the patio to talk. Kiara's dad, Bryce, brought out the pastries and juice, and after nibbling on a few things Katherine did perk up and take on some color. She explained everything the doctors had told her. Stress had been the catalyst to the attack on her adrenal glands, and they'd discovered a tumor in her pituitary gland, which had prompted the emergency surgery. It had been growing in her for possibly decades. She needed to make a lifestyle change. And if so, then her health could be restored.

With the background noise from the street below, tourists walking by and a soft summer breeze listing through her hair, Kiara exhaled and began to relax. Her mom's voice was still confidant, though quieter. She would survive this. Life would move on. Perhaps a bit slower. But for the better.

When her mom placed a palm over the back of Kiara's hand, that surprised her.

"Kiara, you look successful," Katherine said. "Anne Klein, am I right?" she asked, guessing about Kiara's dress. "I read about Kirk Prestige Homes in *Le Monde*. You're picking up the occasional celebrity client. That's helped your visibility. You're a chip off the ol' block—just like your mother."

Kiara nodded but before she could agree with her mom her dad asked, "Are you happy?"

The question of the moment. One that, a week ago, she would have immediately answered *yes*. But now? Bo had changed things. Drastically.

But she lied to herself as she said, "Sure."

Katherine sighed and shook her head. "I know what that *sure* means." Bryce brushed the back of his hand along his wife's cheek. "I used to believe you wouldn't accomplish much with your small-town dreams," her mom continued. "You always wanted the picket fence and the children." She clasped Kiara's hand. "Then when you… Well, you pivoted to the fast track and becoming—" another heavy sigh "—just like me."

"What's wrong with wanting to emulate my mom? I love you, Mom. You've taught me how to be strong and powerful in business. You take what you want and won't let anyone bring you down no matter the emotional cost—" Kiara bit off those last two words too late.

Yes, there had been an emotional cost. To her. Growing up in her mother's absent shadow had allowed Kiara to easily shut down her heart and turn into the controlled Queen of Luxury Real Estate. She was proud of the business accomplishment. But not the manner in which it had been attained. Or rather, the catalyst to that climb to the top. Which had been that night she had run away from Bo and her future.

"And look where that's gotten me," Katherine said wearily. "Brought down by my own inability to deal with that strength and power. I handed my phone over to your dad last night.

The next two weeks are strictly vacation. Healing. Then I have to close my business. It's time, Kiara. Time to start enjoying life before I don't have a life."

"I think that's a good idea." Taken by the urge to claim what she'd desired for decades, Kiara leaned in to hug her mom. She could feel her mother's initial resistance, then she relented. "I'm glad you're slowing down," Kiara said. "I'm sure Dad is, too."

"Maybe?" he joked.

Katherine's laugh was a ghost of her usual confident chuckle. "You'll get used to me being around."

That her parents, who had been married forty years, had to adjust to being around one another crushed Kiara's heart. Sure, they had been happy with their chosen lifestyle. But had they missed so much because of their work and constant separation?

Kiara had never dreamed of a life like that. But her mom was right. She was headed in the very same direction as Katherine Kirk. Hell, she didn't even have a partner with whom to share her fast life. Who would want to step into a frenzied lifestyle like that?

"Kiara?" her dad asked. "How have you been? What's your latest sale?"

He always like to hear about the big price tags

and the crazy, over-the-top houses that million-aires and billionaires spent their money on. "A chateau in Marseille for sixty million euros. It had a helicopter pad and a live-in bartender."

"That's crazy. People spend so much on such insignificant things."

Her dad could live in a cabin and hunt for his own food, and be happy.

"That they do, Dad. But it is good for my business. And it's not insignificant. Houses are for families. Lives are lived, families grow and flourish because of what I do."

"That is meaningful, K-K. You should be proud of your work. But you still live in that little apartment?"

"It's just a stopover."

"Stop it, Kiara," her mother said softly. "Don't be me. My advice has changed, and I want you to listen carefully. Slow. Down."

"I…" *Want to.* "Will think about it."

"I know what that means. It means you'll file it away and never let it surface because you're too busy to care about your own happiness. Work doesn't make a person happy," Kather-ine said.

Same thing Bo had said to her. But not so genuine coming from Katherine Kirk.

"You used to say work was everything." Kiara had once even believed her mother's work

meant more to her than her own daughter. Had a brush with death changed her mother's thinking so dramatically?

"Once, it was. But I've watched you over the years. You've emulated me. Don't do that, Kiara. I've…" She sighed. "I'm sorry, Kiara. I've done some soul-searching since this diagnosis and realize I did a lot of things wrong with you."

"Don't say that, Mom. You did what you believed was right. And look at me. I'm no worse for wear. Quite successful, even."

"You are. And I am very proud of your success. But I wasn't there for you when you needed me most. When you learned about not being able to have children."

Kiara clasped her mom's hand. A squeeze from her said more than any words could.

"I should have never put down your dreams to have a family," Katherine said. "If you want to have a meaningful life you need to put yourself first. And that doesn't mean you stop being CEO. It means seeking happiness and enjoying that. Learn how to incorporate the two."

"Your mom speaks from experience." Her dad leaned across the table and gave her the suspicious eye that he'd used often when she'd been in high school. "You got a man in your life?"

"Actually, I do. But I'm not sure how long it will last. It's Bowen James."

"The fighter? You were so in love with him," Dad said. Then his smile dropped. "But you did have a tough time of it after you ran from that relationship."

"It wasn't because of anything Bo did," Kiara said. "I understand that now."

Bryce nodded. "I'm glad you landed on that understanding. And you see? You couldn't stay away from him. It was meant to be."

Bo had given her all the hints that they should be in a long-term relationship but hadn't come right out and said it. Had she scared him? Was her lifestyle too much for him and his new family? Of course, it was.

"But...he has a baby," she offered quietly.

Katherine arched an eyebrow. "Where's the mother?"

"She died giving birth. She and Bo were never together. It was..." A Heartbreaker thing. Bo's MO. Her parents knew about his press. "What Bo and I have now feels..." *Right.* "I don't know..."

"Do you love him?" her dad asked.

Kiara nodded.

Her mom squeezed her hand again. "If I've taught you anything it's that you have to take what you want. If you don't, then you'll regret it."

"Sounds predatory."

"Sounds like if you don't tell him you love him, he'll never know. And Kiara, I'm sure the idea of stepping in on a situation with another woman's baby troubles you."

"It does. I mean, I think it does. I'm not sure how to feel about Emily. She's so...adorable."

"Well, just because you can't give birth to a child, does not mean you can't give love to one."

Kiara met her mom's eyes. And in that moment, she felt a strange connection to a woman who had always been distant, yet still a remarkable role model. Her mother was telling her she loved Kiara, in the only way she could.

"Thanks, Mom. I needed to hear that."

The three of them clasped hands. Kiara's life would never again be the same.

The next afternoon, Katherine and Bryce Kirk kissed Kiara and left for the azure waters of Greece. Since Katherine's life demanded she stop work, she and her husband had decided it was time to relocate out of the States and move someplace closer to their daughter. London appealed to both of them. So after the Greek vacation, Kiara had a new set of house-hunting clients.

Kiara had barely walked into the courtyard in front of her building when the entrance door buzzed behind her. With a sigh, she turned and opened it to find Bo. And strapped across his chest was Emily, who burbled at the sight of Kiara. The bumblebee cap she wore had a bee-wing propeller. Kiara gave it a flick. "The kid gets in anytime. But you need a password."

He leaned in and nuzzled his nose along her cheek, landing below her ear with a kiss and a lash of his tongue to tickle her earlobe.

"Got it on the first try," she said and then led the twosome up to her apartment.

"Man, this place never gets any bigger," Bo commented as he walked inside. "We have to find you a more spacious place."

"A fridge box?"

"You know it. How did it go with your mum and dad?"

"Actually? It was life-changing."

Bo's brow rose.

"My mom is slowing down. Like a major slowdown. She's quitting her work. And she and dad want to move to London."

"Wow, that's huge."

"It makes me happy. And I recognize that happiness and... I want more."

He took her hand and studied her gaze. "There is something bright about you today. I like it."

She shrugged. "Some of the old Kiara has clawed her way up through the ashes. You were the one who unearthed her." She kissed Emily's head. "She's so content wrapped against you like that. And always taking everything in. She's precious."

"She'll be wanting a bottle soon." Bo set down the backpack that he stocked with all the baby accoutrements. "So before she does, I want to give you this." Bo handed Kiara a folded piece of paper.

"What's this?"

"It's from Emily. Right, Chicken?" He smoothed a palm over his daughter's head. "She dictated while I wrote it down for her during the flight here."

Kiara pressed the paper to her lips. "She's a very smart little girl."

"Much smarter than her dad. Go ahead. Read it."

Unfolding the paper, there were a few short paragraphs in Bo's tiny, tight handwriting. She started to read...

Dear Kiara Kirk,
My daddy told me my first mommy came to this world so she could make sure I got here all right. Then she went to heaven. Daddy says it's a nice place. And I love my daddy. He spoils me. He would give me the world, if he could. We make a good team.

Our team would be perfect if we had one more person on it. Daddy says that makes a family. I think you're pretty, and very gentle with me. And I know you love children. I also know your heart was broken. I think I can help it heal.

Will you be my mommy, pretty please?

A tear splattered on the paper. Kiara pressed the note to her chest, where, indeed, her heart had broken years ago. But it was also the place where Emily now resided.

"So what do you think?" Bo asked. He turned so Emily's face was close to Kiara.

The infant's eyes were wide and searching. It was as though she could see inside her, and Kiara could completely believe she had told Bo exactly what to write.

She kissed Emily's nose, and when the baby reached for her hair and leaned forward, she gratefully took her into her arms.

"I already love you," she said to Emily. "Daddy's little Chicken." The baby conformed to her, snuggled her sweet-smelling head up under Kiara's chin. "And I've been thinking about something since talking to my mom."

"Yeah?" Bo asked.

"Yes. My future. And what I want from it. I've decided that I know what I want in life.

And it's to get back that dream I once had. But I only want that dream if I can share it with the two of you." Kiara lifted her chin and composed herself. Then she asked, "Bowen James, will you marry me?"

Bo's surprised gape made her want to laugh but she tried to maintain her composure. Because, come on, this was a serious moment.

"Can you do that?" he asked. "Ask me to marry you?"

"Why not? What do you mean, Bo?"

"I thought it was always supposed to be the guy who asked?"

"Oh. Well, I'm not your average woman. You need to know that."

"I do know that. I guess I shouldn't have expected anything less from the boss lady. Okay, your proposal stands. But there's just one thing."

Feeling her lip wobble, Kiara couldn't imagine what kind of protest he could offer. Had she made a mistake?

Bo went down on one knee before her and pulled a ring box out of his pocket. "I bought this when I was in New York for the fight." He opened the box to reveal a big sparkler.

Kiara gasped. Smoothed a palm over Emily's head. "You did not."

"I did."

"But I—"

"Doesn't matter what went down then. It changed us both. And I believe it had to happen that way. I knew then you were the woman with whom I wanted to spend the rest of my life. Nothing's changed. Except that we know what's involved in making a real connection this time around. And we've both settled into ways that make us happy. We'll have to learn to adjust to those shared ways—"

"I want to slow down," Kiara interrupted. "I won't become my mother. I want to be a real family, Bo. Not work as much. I can do a lot of work from home. I wouldn't dream to walk into this new family without making that change. Emily deserves it. And so do you."

"I can deal with that. Will you move into the country house with us?"

"Of course! You know I love that place. It felt like I belonged there."

"Yes! Together, we'll make it a home."

Kiara laughed, which prompted Emily to inspect her face with her big blue eyes. "You want me to marry your daddy, Emily?"

Emily's timing couldn't have been more perfect. She giggled and reached out with her fingers, grasping Kiara's hair.

"I think that's a yes." Bo hugged the two of them. "We're going to be a family."

"Yes, we are."

Three weeks later...

Kiara slid into Bo's red convertible. They'd just left Emily at his mom's place for the weekend. The moving company had delivered all of Bo's things to the chateau the day before. They intended to move in and start building the home the three of them desired. And in the process, Kiara would move her stuff from the Paris apartment there as well. Because they'd said vows at the Caen city hall this morning, with Madeline James and her boyfriend as witnesses.

They'd tied the knot! And Kiara had never felt happier.

Yes. She was really happy.

Bo navigated the car around the curved drive and toward the paved road before his mother's property. He paused before turning onto the main road and looked over at her.

"I love you," he said.

"I love you," she challenged back.

Bo turned and propped his elbow on the seat behind him. "Is that how it is, then?"

"You know it, Heartbreaker."

"Well, all right." He flicked on the radio. On the ride to his mom's house, he'd put in Emily's playlist. It was already Kiara's favorite. "Let's do this!"

The Ferrari tore out onto the road. The children's tune "Baby Monkey" bounced out from the speakers. Bo sang along. And Kiara lifted her arms high and shouted in joy.

* * * * *

If you enjoyed this story, check out this other great read from Michele Renae

Cinderella's Second Chance in Paris

Available now!